Catharsis

The Unleashing of the Unconscious
Conflicts of Michael Anthony

To Janet; thank you for your support.

[signature] 06-2017

MICHAEL TYLER

PAGE PUBLISHING, INC.
New York, NY

First originally published by Page Publishing, Inc. 2016

ISBN 978-1-68409-684-8 (Paperback)
ISBN 978-1-68409-685-5 (Digital)

Printed in the United States of America

The following pages are for Lena and Bill.

Contents

Part I
Breakaway

Have you ever been (have you ever been) to Electric Ladyland?
The magic carpet waits for you
So don't you be late
Oh, I wanna show you the different emotions
I wanna run to the sounds and emotions
Electric woman waits for you and me
So it's time we take a ride
We can cast all of your hang-ups over the seaside
While we fly right over the love-filled sea
Look up ahead, I see the love land
Soon you'll understand
Yeah, yeah, yeah

Make love, make love, make love, make love.

I wanna show you
The angels will spread their wings, spread their wings
I wanna show you
Good and evil lay side by side while electric love penetrates the sky
I wanna show you
Lord, Lord, I wanna show you
I wanna show you
Hmmm, hmm, hmm
I wanna show you
Show you
I wanna show you

—Jimi Hendrix, "Have You Ever Been (To Electric Ladyland)"

CHAPTER I

The Awakening

Can you smell it? You, I'm talking to you! Yeah, you. Can you smell it? The paper in your hand? Can you smell it? That faint musty Old Spice fragrance mixed with a dash of indelible black India ink. Man, it reminds me of how I started. You know, how I started writing this thing you're reading—my autobiography. Hey, every word of it is true, but sometimes, I even have trouble believing it. It was like a dream. A fanciful fantasy that started out real enough but hasn't ended. That's right, it hasn't ended! So I decided to write it all down on paper before I forget how it began and all the parts between then and now.

How did it begin? Oh yeah! It's been a long time, but I can still picture the rain. Yes, the rain! The rain came furiously down as the wind blew all round while I made my way haphazardly toward the brightly glowing object some distance away. I was cold and feverish, but I knew that my struggling was not in vain. Somehow I'd make it. Although the strength that once lived robustly within me had gone, leaving me weak and no match against this hostile wind and its furious friend, the rain, I pressed my body hard against the ground and struggled onward. *This is unreal!* I thought for a moment, but only for a moment, for the cold, the wind, and the rain reminded me of the reality of it all. I would raise my head occasionally to see where I was in relation to the glowing object. I felt compelled to reach it. This last time, I saw that I was almost close enough to touch it. Shortly afterward, I noticed that the wind and the rain weren't as violent.

I struggled onward. To what, I knew not. But one thing was clear, I was determined to get there—*here*. After pulling my tired body a few feet more, I began to hear a steady, piercing sound that grew louder by the second as the wind and rain were coming to a halt. Although I had not moved an inch for some time, I noticed the glowing object moving toward me. I wanted to run away, but I didn't have the strength and that piercing sound was just too much. I let out a scream in anguish.

At first everything was hazy, but shortly thereafter, my vision was back to normal and I could see that I was in a cage of some kind. I tried sitting up, but for the lack of strength, I couldn't. I could just barely control the movement of my arms and legs. After a while, I began to think of how it all started, hoping that I could somehow understand what was happening.

Out of the silence, I began to hear footsteps. It wasn't long before the smiling faces of a man and a woman appeared, gazing down at me. At first I thought they were giants, and I didn't know what to do. But after hearing them speak, I did nothing except cry like a—

"Ooh, Mama's baby hungry?" she asked with outstretched arms, as if to strangle me.

As the days faded into weeks and the weeks flowed into months, so went my memory, like a raindrop against some speeding car windshield. I was the typical 1950s baby-booming brat—unwanted, spoiled, and full of good karma and bad TV. I think I was five years old when the light came back on. My memory was restored.

"Hey, man, take a look outside and see what's hap'ning," a disembodied voice whispered into my ear. I rose from my bed, brushing the fog from my eyes and covers from my path to set my feet upon a cold wooden floor. It was day. White light flooded my room from the window. Looking out past the Venetian blinds, I saw *them*. They were dark-complexioned little people (not aliens). I don't mean midgets. They were more like the height of gnomes or fairies. They stood motionless before a huge brightly glowing sphere that appeared to hover gently just inches above the ground.

"Mama, come here. I got the moon in my hands. I got the moon in my hands!" I loudly exuded exuberant exultations of my once lost knowledge while sitting upright on my bed nude; my hands and arms were outstretched as if holding something. It wasn't long before the smiling faces of my father and mother appeared, gazing down at me. My folks thought I was crazy. It didn't take much to shut me up after realizing their attitude, but I remembered what had been revealed to me by *them—truth*. I remembered! Aside from the occasional visitation from *them* and me being abandoned by my parents and reared by my grandparents, I would say that I had the typical childhood living in a moderately large southern city during the 1950s. I was angry a lot of the time.

CHAPTER II

Fly Away

Drifting down from the heavens on a beautiful summer's day to the fair and fairly diligent metropolis of Richmond in the gloriously glamorous commonwealth of Virginia was a very black, jagged tiny piece of powdery substance, consisting mostly of carbon—*soot*. Although it seemed to be an ordinary piece of soot, it wasn't. This piece of soot was far from ordinary, for it was on a mission to find me. I, at that time, was no longer the young black child who was mostly misunderstood by my family. I was a tall, handsome, intelligent, and strong twenty-year-old man, home from the war after being honorably discharged from a two-year tour of active duty in the United States Marine Corps.

I was visiting my foster father and dearest friend, Bill Woodruff, at his perfectly square, plant-filled office. Bill was a psychologist, and I, at the time of our first meeting, was a misunderstood and slightly mixed-up juvenile delinquent (adolescent, for you nonfifties folk). As we spoke fondly of past experiences, I could sense a strangeness in the air. No, I hadn't silently flagellated while sitting across from him. He obviously noticed the faraway look on my face for he asked, "Mike, are you in there?"

"What, what did you say?" I responded slowly. "Did you say something?"

"Yes. I asked if you would mind if I close the window? You don't seem all here for some reason. Where is your mind?" It was déjà vu. I knew every word of the conversation before it was uttered. It was wild, but I went with the flow.

"Ah, yeah, go right ahead and close it. You know, it's funny, but for a beautiful summer's day, it got a bit chilly—no, cold—in here suddenly," I spoke haphazardly.

Just as he was about to close the window, a gust of wind chilled us both. Unbeknown to me then, more than cold air blew in through the open window. That small jagged-edge piece of carbon (soot) drifted in and landed gently on my shoulder unnoticed.

"Ahhh! That's better, don't you think?" stated Bill as he returned to the large cushy black leather chair that stood patiently behind his desk awaiting him. "That's a nice ring you're wearing. Where did you get it?" he asked.

"I got it while in Cali, just before coming home to Richmond," I said while admiring my birthday gift to me—a solid platinum band with the symbol of Pisces. I glanced down at my watch and noticed that I was late for my date with Barbara. Hurriedly, I rose from my seat and said, "Man, I got to go. I was supposed to pick up Barbara five minutes ago."

"Barbara, is it now? When did you meet her?" he queried with a smile as he got up from his chair.

"A friend of mine, Larry, introduced me to her yesterday," I replied while he walked with me toward the door. "I'll call you tomorrow, okay? I want you to listen to Coltrane's latest album."

"Sure, why don't you bring it to the house Sunday and bring Barbara. You two can stay for dinner too," he said as he extended his hand for a friendly handshake and a loving fatherly embrace.

"Yeah, you're on! I'll, I mean we'll, see you Sunday." As I spoke I saw love and pride in his eyes for me. It felt good! I felt good as I walked out the door.

I left the large, overbearing, overpriced office building and proceeded up Broad Street looking for a taxicab. As I walked, I mumbled to myself, "She's going to hate me for being late."

"More than you can ever imagine," a soft, sweet, feminine voice commented.

After taking two steps more, I stopped and turned around to see who said that. When I didn't see anyone in the crowd that I recognized, I continued to walk on. The same voice spoke again. "If you seek the one who speaks, look on your shoulder."

"Who said that?" For a moment I could plainly see the faces of my parents as they appeared that very night when I received my revelation at the age of five years. The people about me looked at me as if I were crazy.

The voice repeated, "Look on your shoulder!" This time I hesitantly obeyed. I looked to both of my shoulders and saw nothing but a tiny piece of soot. I just couldn't figure out who had spoken to me. Was this some joke?

I was about to brush the piece of soot away when the voice screamed, "Don't do that! It is I, the heart of Young Girl Sunday Blues, Summer's daughter, and I have taken the form of a piece of soot. I have journeyed too far to be brushed aside." I looked around one more time to see who might be playing this joke on me when I realized that the people passing me by didn't seem to hear what I had heard. "Now do you believe me?" the voice spoke gently. "You are not crazy nor are you hearing things. It is just that I am communicating to you mentally. I even have the power of letting you listen to your thoughts."

"If you, whoever you are, can do that, I'll believe you." Then I distinctly heard what I, at that moment, was thinking. *Are you shittin' me? There has to be someone somewhere playing this joke on me. Is this* Candid Camera *?*

As I turned completely around, looking at people to see if anyone had heard, the voice spoke, "Now do you believe me?"

I snorted, "I'll be a son of a bitch!"

"I can hear your thoughts, so there is no need for you to speak aloud. Just think of what you wish to say. That's it. The reason why is simple. I was sent here to bring you back with me so that you might search for Rosen Forest."

Rosen Forest. Yeah, I remember them *mentioning this place— Rosen Forest,* I thought.

The voice intruded upon my thinking. "There is more, but you will learn soon enough. As for now, it is time to go."

I wondered how we were going to wherever it was we were going and where was this Rosen Forest place and did it have TV, when suddenly I felt myself rising off the ground, floating upward. The people all round me began to stare in amazement. Some even pointed their fingers and shouted for the police. As if the police could do something other than look. It was wild. I was scared as I slowly ascended above the buildings. But as I became more comfortable with my state, I became less frightened and my assent became more rapid. At one point, I even got cocky. I was traveling and I didn't much give a damn how or where.

"Hey, out of curiosity, what's enabling me to fly?" I asked.

"You are not flying. You are floating. It's the only way you can travel through the DCBA -25."

I thought, *What the hell is the difference, and what is this DCBA-25?*

"Michael, floating is to rise above, flying is to flee, and the DCBA-25 is where one may see the people of the world, what they are, and what they could become. We are passing through now. Look down and you shall see."

I saw an island below us where once was Virginia. The voice told me that it was the Island of Theorists and Stylists, commonly known as the Land of Troublemakers. As I stared down at the island, I saw people speaking to others through loud speakers. There were people such as Richard "The Milhouse" Nixon, Eldridge Cleaver, Paul Rupert, Rennie Davis, the Reverend Cotesworth Lewis, Sharon Krebs (rudely in the nude), Ernest Che Guevara (on 20-20 with Geraldo), Arsenio "The Man" Hall, and so many others. It wasn't funny. But around the island was a purple sea of people—the same people—cooperatively living, learning, and loving together.

"Hey, that's heavy, but what do the letters DCBA-25 mean?"

Her sweet gentle voice entered my mind softly and said, "Decadent Charismatic Bourgeois Aristocrats minus Twenty-Five Percent of Reality. They are a bunch of jerks who really just want to live the good life in Buenos Aires."

We continued to travel upward until we came to a cloud that was just above what the voice called the Sun of Reality. There we stopped. The voice told me to sit and rest for a while. The piece of soot gently left my shoulder and floated around to confront my face. I was eyeball to soot.

"Michael, it is time for me to leave you, for you must find your way to Rosen Forest from here. But as you travel remember this: no matter how beautiful things may seem, you must not stay in any place too long. The lands through which you will travel are not your destination. I must go. Remember what I said." Her words reverberated as the speck of soot faded into nothingness.

CHAPTER III

The Search for Rosen Forest Begins

I stared in fear and wondered what the hell I were to do. I looked around in bewilderment only to find nothing but whiteness. In which direction do I head? I shook my head and exclaimed aloud, "What have I gotten myself into now?"

Wait a minute. She said rest. I pondered for a moment. "Yeah, that's what I need—rest. Yeah, sleep!" I began to feel woozy and tired. "I think I had better lie here for a while before I go anywhere. Why do I feel so dizzy and sleepy? What's happening to me? I feel as if I'm going to black out. What the hell is happening? I can't see. It's just black. Wait, my eyes are closed. I'll just open them. They won't open. This is a dream—a bad dream. Wait a minute Mike, get control of yourself. All I have to do is open my eyes and wake up. That's all, just get control. It's all a dream. Yes, that's all this is, a dream. And all I have to do is just wake myself up. I am going to open my eyes and wake myself up. Wake up, dammit!"

When I finally opened my eyes, I wished I hadn't. I saw that I was inside something, but I wasn't. I couldn't understand the madness that was happening to me. It was a trip! I was surrounded by something. Bright, vibrant colors were flashing on and off, wild, whirling colorful designs whizzing by my face, and unusual sounds and vibrations entering my ears and shaking my body.

All of a sudden I realized that I was moving. I was more or less being drawn toward something, like a magnet attracts metal. What it was that was pulling me, I didn't know. I felt that I must have been getting closer to it because I was moving faster and faster. Then suddenly, upon the vast horizon of colors and shapes, I could see it, but I still couldn't identify it. I was headed straight for it and moving faster by the moment. I screamed in exasperation, "Help-p-p-p-p!"

"Ouch!" I yelled, while simultaneously swinging my right hand across my body to kill whatever it was that stung me. "Wait a minute, Mike. If I'm dead, why the hell did I say ouch? I must be dead. I have to be. Otherwise I couldn't have lived through all that, whatever it was. I'm no superman. All I have to do is open my eyes—my eyes are open!" I jumped to my feet, and to my surprise, I found myself in a vast beautiful field full of beautifully colored flowers that looked like tilted square plates that were a rainbow of cool colors. Each flower had a different design on it. The smell was sweet and unlike anything I had ever experienced. I was surrounded by what seemed to be long-haired, head-banded hippies.

"Is this Woodstock?" I wondered aloud. Their faces slowly smiled at me. It was then that I realized they were nude! Shortly after that brainstorm, it dawned on me that I too was without clothes. At that very moment, a lovely little girl about the age of seven emerged from the surrounding crowd of hippies. She held a bunch of the beautiful flowers in her hand. As she walked toward me, she uttered the words, "Peace and love," repeatedly while offering me her flowers. I was dumbfounded. When she reached me, she laid the flowers at my feet and kindly took hold of my hand to lead me back to her people. I followed obediently.

"Daddy Wong Legs, commonly called Clarence, has sent me for you," she said as we walked pass the sea of gently smiling hippie faces.

She caught me off guard for a moment. Her little voice penetrating the sweet smelling air helped me realize that this was real. "What is your name?" I asked.

"Myxolydia is what I am called," she said while looking up at me with a smile. "Now you must not talk anymore."

We stopped just a few feet beyond the crowd. I looked around to see nothing but green grass before us, upon which she fell to her knees and clapped her hands twice. Before I could blink an eye, I found myself alone in an attractively decorated and spacious room. There were no windows nor did there appear to be a door. "How did I get here?" I thought aloud. Lying on a beautiful king-sized bed made of ebony wood were clothes. The pants were jet black with a multicolored, tie-died, frilly shirt that looked like waves were going across it. I thought for a moment that the shirt was a bit feminine, but I brushed the thought aside because I needed the clothes and Sears was not in the neighborhood. As I dressed, my mind began to wonder if this was some type of cage, why was I brought here, and how do I get out.

"You may leave in peace whenever you wish," a commanding voice stated. I was startled and became defensive while looking for the owner of the voice but found no one. Before I could get acquainted with this room, I found myself standing in the middle of another much larger room that was lavishly decorated with baroque furnishings. I didn't let down my guard for a minute. I moved slowly and cautiously around the room while admiring the ornate beauty of the furniture. Without warning the voice spoke again, "I am Daddy Wong Legs, the great prophet, commonly called Clarence. Who are you?"

I turned around quickly and found an old man suspended in midair in the lotus position. He looked like death warmed over. This dude was old! It appeared to me that every visible hair on his body was white and his brown skin was as wrinkly as one of those ugly Chinese bulldogs. But where did he come from? He wasn't there when I scanned the room moments ago, and how is he able to levitate like that?

I began with, "I've got a few questions…"

"Come closer and tell me who you are," he said in a commanding but gentle tone.

"Look, my name is Michael Anthony and I'm supposed to be on my way to—"

"Silence! I have heard enough. No, this is not the place you seek. Come, sit beside me." Before I knew it, I was sitting beside him, levitating, and we were in an entirely different room. This room was Spartan and spacious.

"How did you do that?" I asked.

"How one does a thing is not as important as why one does a thing but enough of that. Michael, your name means 'godlike.' Did you know this?" He didn't let me answer. "It is of no matter. You are from the Apex of Reality, and you are on an embryonic journey to meet Summer's daughter."

"How did you know?"

"I just know, my son. I also know that you have spent too much time here. We will feed you and you may rest here in my domain for twenty-four hours, but then you must be on your way."

CHAPTER IV

Fatima, Everybody's Next One

Just as I was about to ask a question, I found myself in what appeared to be a dining room. I was sitting at a rather large oak table and sitting across from me was a very beautiful young lady. On the table before me were two glasses with some type of amber colored, sweet-smelling liquid in them. I couldn't take my eyes off her.

"I trust you will enjoy your meal. Please drink, it will sustain you for eighty hours." Her voice was mellifluous and enchanting.

After drinking both glasses of liquid, I asked, "Who are you and what happened to Clarence?"

She smiled at me as she spoke. "Is that all you wish to ask? You had so many questions for Clarence."

"Well, don't you think those two are enough to start with?"

I hardly noticed the change of scenery from dining room to another beautiful field of strange flowers, and this time I was standing. These flowers were a different shape, looking like upside down tiny teacups. Each flower was a solid translucent color of the rainbow. When my eyes found her, she was sitting on the grass looking up at me and beckoning me to come sit beside her. She was an angel! Her clear caramel complexion and sweet-smelling long wavy auburn hair captivated me.

She took my hand and whispered, "Come and place your head on my lap. Relax while I explain." I did as she bade. "I am Clarence's daughter, Everybody's Next One, commonly called Fatima. Clarence is always busy. This is why I am explaining things to you. You are a beautiful young man." I smiled and picked a blue flower and stuck it in her hair, as she continued. "You are in the Land of the Lotus and I and my people are called Cruds. The city we live in is called Mazeze."

As she talked about her people and the people who lived to the south in the city called Desperation, the Everyday People, I became totally immersed in her mellifluous voice and voluptuous beauty. Reality, for me, was the two of us under a clear blue-green sky. "Michael, you are so beautiful. I want you to kiss me. Please?" I sat up and gazed into her hazel eyes for a moment. As I caressed her cheeks with my hands, I sensed some anxiety from her. She slipped her arms around my waist as I kissed her soft, warm lips.

Suddenly she broke away from my embrace and stood up. I looked up at her in wonder. "Come, let us walk along the field of flowers," she said as she looked away uneasily. "Our people are in danger. The Everyday People do not live nor believe in peace and love as we do. They want to kill us because we are different in our beliefs." She appeared distant.

I asked, "Why did you want me to kiss you? And what are you really thinking about, your people or what just took place between you and me?"

She turned and fell to her knees before me and with the look of "forgive me" on her face, she said, "I don't understand my emotions. I have never felt this way before, and as for what I am thinking about, well, my thoughts are on me and how alone I will feel when you are gone. I know I shouldn't feel or think this way, but I do."

"As long as you live you must think and feel what you want because it's part of living." I smiled. "A very dear friend told me that and now I'm telling you."

She reached out to me with one hand, and with a smile on her face she said in a soft way, "Speak to me of love and love me."

I took her hand and pulled her close to me. She whispered softly in my ear, "Thank you!" The flowers embraced us as we made passionate love.

I opened my eyes sometime later to find her asleep beside me and the moon shining its light upon our nude bodies. I woke her with a kiss. She smiled and said as she reluctantly got to her feet, "It is time for me to return alone to my father and my people. If you were to return with me, I would not let you leave me because I truly love you. I must leave you now while I still have the emotional strength to fight." She disappeared before I could stop her. As I rose to my feet, I heard her say, "I will always be your plastic, fantastic lover." I called out to her asking her to return, but she was gone. Sadly I walked on, not knowing where I was going or what to expect when the morning came.

CHAPTER V

Odori and Whew

The morning sun found me standing atop a rocky cliff overlooking the vast expanse of a red sea. After standing there, marveling at the sunrise and watching the waves crash against the rocks, I noticed a girl sitting on a rocky perch jetting out from the cliff some fifty feet below me. I was hypnotized by the sight of her. I couldn't see her face, but I wanted her to be Fatima. She wore a red sarong and a pink scarf wrapped loosely around her head. I stood there, not thinking, as I watched her slowly rise and jump from her precarious resting place. I even watched in disbelief as her body crashed into the cresting waves below. It all appeared to happen in slow motion. After recovering from my bewilderment, I dove in after her, still hoping that she was Fatima. I searched for her under the waves. In my searching, I forgot my need for air and passed out.

For those of you who have nearly drowned, you can empathize with my rude awakening. The vomiting, water was coming out of my mouth, nose, and eyes at the same time. The gasping for breath, I didn't know which way was up. The headache and the stomachache that tells you it's time for something more than an Alka Seltzer. I was hurting!

"Welcome back to the living!" I heard, while being tossed onto my knees by some rubbery thing. While kneeling, coughing, vomiting, and hurting from head to toe, I heard, "Come now, you're going to be all right."

"Who the hell is that, and how would you know, you're not puking," I said between coughs while attempting to stand and focus my eyes. After getting my balance and sight back to normal, I saw that I was inside a huge bubble under the sea. The bubble was almost clear but had a very light greenish-yellow tint. The shock of realizing where I was knocked me on my ass. I panicked!

"Calm down! Nothing's going to hurt you down here." When I saw her, the girl in the red sarong, outside the bubble, I really freaked. "Get a grip or you will hurt Whew," she said emphatically. I finally calmed myself after realizing that there was nothing to fear. "Hi! I hope you are feeling—"

"Who are you and what is this thing I'm in?" I interrupted in anger.

"Well, my name is Odori and you are inside my friend Whew. Whew is a melanin bubble. There aren't many of them around these days. But enough of me, why did you come here, and who are you?"

I hesitated a bit and then said, "I thought you were in trouble and well, ah, what are you? A girl or a fish?"

"I'm an Auk! There aren't many of us around either. Not many since the Everyday People moved into this area. Their leader, Schizoid Man, hates us Auks because we can live underwater as well as on land. But you didn't tell me your name."

I sat down and placed my head between my legs and said, "Mike! My name is Michael."

"Well, Mike-Michael, where do you want to go? Maybe Whew and I can help," she said smiling.

"I'm searching for Rosen Forest. Do you know the place?" I asked.

She thought for a moment and said, "Nope! I am not familiar with this place, Rosen Forest. Maybe the Great Prophet can help you."

"I've been to the city of Mazeze and I've seen him and he couldn't help me."

"Well, Mike-Michael, you may stay with Whew and me if you want," she said with a smile.

I looked at her like she was crazy when a strange bright orange and blue striped fish approached. This fish attached itself to her forehead with its mouth. I thought she was being attacked. She was motionless for a minute or two, and then the fish detached itself and swam away. A look of worry came over her face and she began to speak in a strange tongue. It wasn't long after that she took off swimming with the bubble and me following. Boy, could she move through the water. It wasn't long before I noticed large schools of fish, of all shapes, sizes, and colors, swimming in the same direction as us.

I yelled to her, "Hey, what's going on? Where are we going?"

She looked back at me and said, "It's not safe. Uncle Schizoid's Misguided Children (USMC) are on the move."

"You mean the Everyday People?"

"Yes, and they are destroying everything in sight. The Cruds will be devastated because they do not believe in fighting," she explained.

"Hey, stop! I can't go with you. I can't leave Fatima!" She stopped, and at that very same moment, the bubble stopped. "I can't leave her. Please let me go?"

She looked at me forlornly and asked, "Are you sure?"

"Yes!"

"Well, Mike-Michael, Whew will take you to Mazeze but no farther." She stroked the side of the bubble and spoke in that strange tongue. The bubble then took off toward the surface. As we headed upward, I heard her voice reverberating from the wall of the bubble. She said, "Take care!"

CHAPTER VI

Return to Mazeze

The bubble burst through the surface of the sea with such force that the resulting wave overturned and sank two of Schizoid Man's battle barges. The bubble continued upward for several minutes before it began to fly toward land and Mazeze. I noticed that the tint changed to match the sky, so we were almost invisible. As we approached Mazeze, I could see massive destruction and death. Mazeze was being reduced to ruin, and its people were being annihilated. The buildings were topless and filled with holes the size of a semi-truck. The ground was covered with rubble and bodies. I could only hope that Fatima was still alive.

The bubble gently landed on a back street near the center of Mazeze. Almost immediately, it began to rise up into the air without me, and as it did, I heard Odori's voice reverberate from the walls of the bubble saying, "Take care!" I watched it fly safely away toward the sea and Odori.

Abruptly, someone ran into the back of me. I looked down to find Myxolydia clinging fearfully to my waist. She was being pursued by a pale, nude man with a long sharp knife. He stopped about five feet from us. Being so frightened, she quickly jumped to the rear of me. The nude man gave a loud laugh and charged wildly at me. I stepped to the right of him as he charged pass, and I followed through with a side kick to the back of his bald head, causing him to run head first into the wall of a large brick building. Needless to say, the poor bastard came to an abrupt and painful conclusion as his head split open and blood poured out onto the ground.

As I watched his body slump into unconsciousness upon the ground beside the building, Myxolydia hastily spoke, while grabbing my hand and heading off at a run in the direction from which she came. "Come, I will take you to Clarence and Fatima. Maybe you can help." I followed quickly at the same pace!

We ran past burning buildings and the dead bodies of innocent people. We dodged big and little explosions and showers of falling debris. We ran up alleyways and down the middle of streets until we finally arrived at a massive pyramid-shaped building that had taken a brutal beating from a bomb barrage. Myxolydia told me that they were inside and needed help badly. The interior of the building left even less to be desired than the exterior. The wall hangings were in shreds, there were huge holes in the walls, and the floor was covered in rubble. When we finally reached them, Fatima was in tears kneeling beside her father, who was pinned down under a massive marble pillar which once held part of the roof. Myxolydia stood in shock. I ran over to see if there was anything I could do, but Clarence had been dead for some time.

"Come, Fatima, there isn't anything we can do for him," I said as she clung to me sobbing.

Suddenly there was the loud explosion of another bomb and the building began to collapse, but Fatima teleported all of us just outside the huge doors of an old stone castle before it was too late. It looked like it had come out of the Middle Ages.

She looked at me and said forcefully, "Go! Go now! Only you can enter the castle without being harmed."

"What are you talking about? I'm not going anywhere without you and Myxolydia."

"No, Michael, I must stay here with my people. They need me, and you must be on your way to Rosen Forest." She held Myxolydia closer to her side and smiled at me through her tears as if to let me know that all would be okay.

"Fatima, Mazeze is destroyed and your people killed," I pleaded. "I can help you. You can come with me. I need you!"

"Michael, those of my people who have survived this day will be on their way to the safety of Shitzo Forest. I will meet them there and we will start anew. I love you, but my destiny is elsewhere. Now go, for you are needed by another."

I kissed her warm luscious pale pink lips and brushed away her tears with my finger in hopes that she would change her mind. She pushed me away and shouted, "Go!" I slowly turned and walked into the castle knowing that I would never see her again. I looked back, but she and Myxolydia were gone.

CHAPTER VII

The Embryonic Journey Continues

I reluctantly entered the castle. As I walked past the massive iron doors, I noticed a faint red throbbing light in the distance. Without realizing it, I became fixed on it as it hypnotized me. After walking a ways, I heard the faint echoes of music. It sounded as if someone was playing a flute.

"Is there someone in here?" I yelled. I paused a moment, waiting for a response. I became consumed in the music. *I'm being drawn toward it*, I thought. Upon getting closer to its source, I saw the faint red light become a curtain of red lights, and I couldn't stop from walking into it. I became apprehensive as I thought, *The music is somewhere beyond the light.*

After passing through the curtain of red lights, I realized that I could see but I couldn't hear and I was nude. I wanted to turn around and go back, but I was compelled to continue on. It was as if my feet had a mind of their own. As I looked around, I saw a small green girl kneeling and playing a flute. She was wearing a colorful poncho and a yellow flower in her dark green hair. Behind her was a large man whose green shade matched hers with his arms spread open as if to welcome me. I could see his words floating in the air as he spoke. He was repeating over and over, "Now is the time to paint this number. A number to paint to pass the time. It is fun to have the time to paint by number."

As I walked pass them, they began to fade into nothingness, and I noticed, softly at first, voices chanting in unison "Rosen Forest" while streams of multicolored lights sped pass me in waves. The lights were making a sound like I had never heard before.

The sights and sounds were dizzying. I had to close my eyes before I passed out.

Upon opening my eyes, after all sensation of movement had ended, I found myself inside a drop of light-blue water, which was falling rapidly but in slow motion toward the ground. Below was a vast field of pink and yellow daisies swaying back and forth in the light of the sun. After hitting the ground and being freed from my prison of water, I got to my feet and started to brush myself off. While brushing the water from my body, I realized that the daisies were larger than me. I was the size of a large ant. As I continued to look around befuddled, I happened to notice a piece of discarded tan cloth, which I picked up and used as a poncho. Soon after, I happened upon a piece of black string, which I tied around my waist and used as a belt. Hey, I didn't get them from Kmart, but it was better than nothing. I only wished I had some BVDs and a pair of K-Swiss to go along with it. And what about a pair of Levis and a gold chain and...

While admiring my tattered, handmade clothes, I realized that I was hungry (my stomach growled, which brought me back to reality). My search for food had begun. It didn't take long, for there in the distance (about seven feet in front of me) was an enormous spider's web. Considering my size, it was enormous. Entangled in the web was a man. The sucker looked to be in a bad way. His bald head and sissy striped blue and white tights with a matching blue shirt weren't the half of it. You see, there was this really big black widow spider making her way toward him from the right hand corner of the web, and I was sure glad I wasn't in his place because she looked hungry. I immediately began to look for a weapon or something with which to kill or distract the spider. Believe me, I wasn't being heroic or altruistic. I was hungry and maybe this guy could help.

I soon saw a bow and some arrows that obviously belonged to the trapped man. I quickly grabbed the bow and an arrow, took careful aim, and missed the spider. (I'm sure that guy was pissed.) Again I took careful aim and let go an arrow that was true. I hit the bitch. The arrow pierced one of the many eyes of the spider. The spider was in a rage, to say the least. I had upset her dinner plans. She fell to the ground, knocking free the arrow from her eye. It didn't take long for her to focus on me and attack. I grabbed another arrow and shot. The arrow lodged itself in the brain of the arachnid after passing between its poisonous mandibles. I killed the damn thing. Boy, was I relieved. That was the last arrow.

It took me a while to recover, but when I did, I turned my attention toward freeing the man (the spider's dinner). While untangling him, I asked, "What's your name?"

He said nothing, but there was fear and confusion in his eyes.

I smiled and said, "Cat got your tongue? Well, I'll tell you something, slick. If I hadn't come by when I did, that spider would have gotten your tongue and more."

When he was finally free, he sucker punched me and ran off. Now I was pissed and still hungry. I swiftly ran after him. My pursuit brought me to his village. Everyone was dressed as he was. As I walked through the village, the people stared at me in fear. Suddenly the sky went black and all you could hear was a buzzing sound. Almost immediately, the people of the village ran for the safety of their huts, shouting words in a language I had never heard before. The men of the village grabbed their weapons (bows and arrows) and got into position to do battle. Before I really knew what was going on, the enemy had attacked in full force. This was crazy. I wanted to eat not fight. The attackers were women riding the backs of some type of dark red beetle. They were hunting the men of the village. I tried to help the villagers, but it was useless. There were thousands of women and their beetles.

I fought and fought until I was captured. They were tenacious hunters. They cleared the village of its male populous. These nude, rugged women took us to their domain: a tree. They reminded me of those ants that live in trees. They crowded as many of us as would fit into a large wooden cage that hung from one of the branches of the tree. When it was time to eat, I wasn't fast enough. Two of our jailors tossed us scraps of bread and meat, the same way as one would toss popcorn to pigeons in the park. Needless to say, I didn't eat.

Early the next day, two guards came and took me away. They were armed with highly complex weapons (compound crossbows and hunting knives). I asked them if they had been to the local army or navy store. They responded by kicking me in the stomach and hitting the back of my head with the butt of a crossbow. Needless to say, I wasn't hungry anymore.

I quietly and obediently followed them through the maze of passageways to the base of the tree. They led me outside the tree to an upturned paper cup with a hole on its side. When we arrived at the cup, the two guards disdainfully shoved me in through the hole. I stumbled and fell to the floor of the cup. My face landed on the silky smooth abdomen of a beautiful half-nude girl. She giggled. I guess because my nose landed in her sweet-smelling navel.

I raised my head slowly to hear, "So you are the strange one." Her voice was soft and seductive. "Stand up! I want to see just how strange you really are." I did as she commanded, all the while looking for an escape opportunity. "You are strange. You aren't white like the others. You're brown! Where did you come from?"

"If I told you, you wouldn't know. So forget it," I spoke in anger.

The look on her face was one of shock. "Oh! You are strange. You not only talk, but you talk like I. But the big question be, can you please I? Sexually?"

I looked deep into her hazel eyes and asked, "To whom am I speaking?"

"I be Fiaka, Queen of the Beetles. And you, I will—" Just at that moment the cup was knocked over by an enormous bright blue butterfly. "Guards, kill the demon before it kills I," she cried.

The rush of air from the butterfly's wings knocked the guards and me to the ground. Before I knew what was happening, I found myself in the clutches of the butterfly being carried off. As it flew away with me dangling from beneath its body, I could see her vivacious breasts waving good-bye as she yelled at her guards to kill the damn demon and bring me back.

CHAPTER VIII

To Finally Meet Summer's Daughter

I was too weak to resist the will of this creature. All I could think of was eating; both me eating and me being eaten by this thing that couldn't fly straight if its life depended on it. You know, watching a butterfly fly is very different from flying with one. It's a wild and crazy roller-coaster ride. I would have puked had I eaten earlier. After flying for a long time (hours) over sandy deserts and colorful seas, I could see in the distance a beautiful green rainforest. As we approached it, I was surprised to notice that I had begun to regain my normal size and the butterfly had begun to fade away. Just as we entered the forest, the butterfly was no more, and I found myself walking through the pristine beauty of this serene place. As I walked, I noticed my strength returning, and there was a gentle peace that was all around me. I walked without a care of where I was or where I was going. I walked until I came upon a stunning sparkling waterfall. At the base of the waterfall was a silver long-haired haired siren basking in the coolness of the falling water.

She called out to me as if we had been fast friends for years. "Michael, I've been waiting for you. Come closer. I won't bite! Come and eat, you must be hungry."

I walked closer, not knowing what to expect but feeling secure. As I approached her, I could clearly see a violet aura all around her that was extending out into infinity. I sat before her in an ebony chair at a table made of white marble. It was elegance and comfort at its epitome, and all I thought of was food. The table held a spread fit for a king. There were all kinds of fruits, vegetables, meats, and drinks. I wasn't bashful. Remember, I had been on the verge of starving. Between mouthfuls, I asked, "How do you know my name, and where am I?"

She looked at me with a smile and said in a very soft tone, "I am Summer's daughter."

I stopped eating and just looked at her in surprise for a moment. "If you are Young Girl Sunday Blues that means I'm in Rosen Forest. I made it!" I sat back in the chair and sighed. "So that's what you meant by 'I've been waiting for you!'"

"Yes!" I got up from the table and walked to an old oak tree, which was behind me. Before I could ask what was on my mind, she spoke gently to me. "Michael, I know of all the questions on your mind, but I can't answer them because the purpose of your journey has not been completely fulfilled." I asked her what is the purpose of my journey and she replied, "You have to answer that question along with most of your other questions."

In anger, I yelled, "Why?"

For a while the only sound was that of my voice echoing through the forest and then dead silence. She looked at me solidly and told me to have patience. She then rose magnanimously from her seat and sauntered over to me. Placing her hands upon my shoulders, I turned to face her. In a gentle way she said, "Come, Michael, you must eat and then rest. In the morning you will meet someone who needs and wants to be needed, for she does not have the understanding you have."

I asked, "Who? Where? Why me?"

All she said was "In the morning, you must follow your heart until you get to the magic gardens and pleasure fields of life. It is there you will find her. Trust in yourself always. And remember, live and in living follow your heart." And with that she faded into infinity.

CHAPTER IX

Have You Tried Love

When morning came and I opened my eyes, I heard a beautiful hypnotic song of a soul bird. I got to my feet and walked in the direction of the singing. Seconds later, everything disappeared, and I knew that I was on my way to see the girl of whom Summer's daughter spoke. As I traveled through the vast, colorful, timeless, infinite void of the Divine Attribute, I looked on in wonder and amazement. I heard the voices of the universe chanting, "Have you tried love?" Soon afterward, I reached life, a primitive pristine protean of nature's ever-changing whim. I walked until I came to a soft green meadow bordered by a menagerie of sensitive hearts, manifesting themselves in the form of delicate, fragrant white flowers. In the distance I could hear the lovely song of the soul bird, which brought me to this place. Suddenly before me appeared a lovely young lady who seemed unaware of what was happening to her. Her hair was long, black, and silky. Her eyes were green, and her milk chocolate skin looked soft, smooth, and inviting. It seemed as though she couldn't see me until I asked her name.

She was startled at first, then she looked into my eyes, and in a sensuously soft tone asked, "Who are you and where did you come from?"

"I'm Mike. I mean, I'm Michael. Wow. My name is Michael Anthony, and you?"

"My, my, my… I'm Brown Brenda. I mean, Brenda Brown."

We just looked at each other for a moment, and as I looked into her eyes, I knew that I was in love. I just reached over and gently kissed her and said, "Miss Brown, I've found you and I hope you've found me."

From that moment on, life was ours: the sky changed colors each day we were together. We listened to the music of the Ostrich. We remembered the hymns of the Psychedelic Senate of Streetmosse. We rejoiced to the dreams or pax or nepenthe. We breathed orange air. I gave her all of me, it was beautiful, and in turn she gave me her. For the first time in my life, I felt alive. We exchanged ideas, and we shared each other's joy and sadness.

Then one day the sky turned purple and the thunder roared and the lightning flashed all around. The winds from the Land of Sarcasm swept through life in a rage. I realized then that OM, the First Spirit, the vibration, the sound which sets everything else into being, had come to take me away from Brenda and Brenda away from me. I could not allow this to be. I fought OM because I needed, wanted, and loved her. It was the first time I had loved anyone freely and in turn had been loved. But as I fought, I could see everything fading away. I saw her fade away!

I cried out, "Brenda! Don't go, fight it, Brenda. Fight it! Brenda!" I continued to fight, all the time feeling hate for OM. I fought OM until I died inside thinking I had killed OM. "I killed. I killed OM! I… killed… OM," I said in astonishment, realizing what I had truly done. My hate turned to regret as I fell to my knees and cried, "H-el-l-l-l-l-l!" Then I began to see the events of the past but in reverse. "I'm going backward in time? What the hell is happening?" I shouted.

Suddenly there was nothing but darkness. I felt so alone. I opened my eyes and to my surprise I found a white sandy beach beneath my knees. Almost out of nowhere appeared people in bathing suits, children playing, and lovers loving. As I looked around befuddled, I pronounced with glee, "I'm back! I'm in reality, but how?"

Just then I felt a beach ball hit me in the back. I turned around and picked it up and tossed it back to the kids who were playing with it. Without warning, everyone and everything froze and a beam of white light descended from the heavens upon me and a voice spoke. It was Young Girl Sunday Blues. "Look to your right, Michael, and you will see Brenda with someone new to love."

True enough, it was. She was still beautiful and in love but with another. With tears in my eyes and in a sorrowful tone, I asked, "Does she still remember me?"

"Yes, but she has accepted her loss just as you must. You will find love again as you travel through life, so live Michael. Live and have fun, because love is life and if you live life, you will love," she said gently.

The light began to fade away, and as I watched Brenda, I knew the purpose of my journey—to accept, respect, and love completely me. I also knew that this wasn't the end but just the beginning. For *they* had told me long ago—life never ends; it only begins. The beginning!

Part II
The Beginning

When I'm with you
It doesn't matter where we are
Or what we're doing
I'm with you, that's all that really matters
Time passes much too quickly
When we're together laughing
I wish I could sing it to you
I wish I could sing it to you
Mostly I'm silent
Never think about words to say
When I kiss you
I feel a thousand different feelings
The color of chills
All over my body
And when I feel them
I quickly try to decide which one
I should try to put into words
Mostly I'm silent
Only the beginning of what I want to feel forever
Only the beginning
Only just the start
I've got to get you into my life
Got to get you next to me
Only the beginning
Only just a start

—Chicago, "Beginnings"

CHAPTER I

Them Made Me Look, the Dirty Crook

"Hey, man, take a look outside and see what's hap'ning," a voice from the past whispered into my ear. *Them.* The image of a brightly glowing clear sphere appeared to hover gently before my mind's eye. I knew it was *them. Them*, the pervaders of *truth. Them*, who first spoke to me when I was five, spoke to me now as I stood with tears in my eyes while watching Brenda and her new love frolicking in the sun. As the image of the glowing sphere faded into nothingness, I heard, "Go ahead and look. You are going to get into something nice." So I looked, and to my surprise, the surrounding scene had changed.

There I sat in the living room of my grandparent's house, upon my grandmother's brand-new beige Victorian sofa, freshly covered in clear plastic. I sat staring out the picture window on the front of the house, staring at puffy white clouds as they float by, hiding parts of a clear blue sky. Staring at a neighborhood of two-story Victorian homes owned by two-story-minded middle class Negro people. Staring at the occasional unseen, unloved, homeless dog or cat just out for a Sunday afternoon stroll down the street while they stare back at me. Yeah, I realized that I was staring at me staring and daydreaming about what the future will bring, as I often did when I was younger. Daydreaming about why I hadn't done my homework, daydreaming about becoming rich or famously rich or both. Daydreaming about why my parents didn't love me and what it would be like to have a father like Ward Clever on *Leave It to Beaver!* Yeah, that was me in front of the window, daydreaming.

"Michael, your dinner is ready. Come on and eat." It was Nanny and she hadn't changed. There she stood at the doorway to the dining room. Still the same grandmother. Her long black hair (having only a few streaks of gray) was in a French ball and she was wearing that flowery blue apron she always wore on Sunday, which meant crispy fried chicken, tasty potato salad, fresh baby sweet peas, piping hot buttered dinner rolls, and for desert, a deliciously golden slice of pineapple upside down cake. For a minute, I forgot that I was watching what was, as it was when I was eighteen. I became homesick and hungry for things as they were.

"Hey, man, remember, 'If things never change, they will simply stay as they are. But on the other hand, she wore a glove!' Enjoy!" And with that, *them* were gone and the same was true of that Sunday. I looked around baffled as hell to find myself standing on a sandy beach alone. Out of nowhere appeared people in bathing suits, children playing, and lovers loving. *Am I back? Is it over?* I thought.

Just then I felt a beach ball hit me in the back. I turned around and picked it up and threw the red, white, and blue ball back to the young boys who had been playing with it. Suddenly everyone froze and slowly began to turn to sand. At the same time, I noticed that the ocean and the sky turned yellow and the sun changed from gold to blue. "What's happening? I thought this was the end of the journey. Where am I now? Am I going crazy? Will someone help me please?"

Scared and confused, I began to walk around looking at the people. I was startled at first when the people began to walk around as if they were blind, but they seemed to be headed in the same direction, so I followed. I had followed them for some minutes when I heard a woman scream for help. Shortly after I heard the scream, I noticed that the people had stopped marching and had begun to merge together to form a wall of sand. I was completely baffled. I began to run ahead of the crowd to see who had screamed and hopefully get some answers. I had run no more than fifty feet when I stopped to see an enormous red, white, and blue metallic eagle soaring about a hundred yards away from my location atop a very large sand dune. Directly under the eagle, on the ground, a girl was running and screaming for help. I began to run toward her at breakneck speed. As I ran to her aid, I felt a slight shocking sensation, and as I got closer the sensation became stronger until it got to the point where I screamed in pain, but I couldn't stop. I closed my eyes and refused to let the pain hinder me from my goal. I collided into the girl with such force that we were both stunned.

CHAPTER II

Possession

I have found myself atop many a beautiful woman in my day, but never have I had a headache because of it. Upon opening my eyes and finding her beneath me, I tried to wake her, but she was out cold, down for the count, dead to the world, unconscious. After gazing upon her beauty, I looked around for the eagle. When I spotted it, it was returning for both of us. I quickly got to my feet, picking her up. As I did, I noticed that the eagle's eyes began to glow orange. Just as I took off running with her in my arms, a multicolored ray was emitted from both eyes of the eagle. The ray struck the ground about two feet in front of us, turning the sand into molten hot glass. I quickly stopped, turned to my left, and dodged behind a very large bolder which just happened to be in the right place at the wrong time. I knew that it didn't offer me any real protection against this flying nightmare, but it might give me some time to think of a way out.

Just as the eagle passed over us, it emitted a second ray which struck the bolder and disintegrated it. As I watched the eagle turn and head back in my direction, I knew it would not miss this time. I looked down at her and whispered, "I'm sorry," when suddenly there on the ground beside her voluptuous thighs appeared an M79 grenade launcher and an AG round. At first I was reluctant to pick them up, but I quickly grabbed the launcher, breach loaded the AG round, aimed, and fired. Just as I fired, I saw the eagle's eyes begin to glow and two seconds later—*boom*. It was a direct hit between the eyes.

I fell to my knees in relief, but just as I did, the M79 disappeared, and before I knew what had happened, I found myself in total, absolute darkness. I felt along the ground for the girl, but she was nowhere to be found. I got to my feet and screamed, "What the hell is this, goddammit?"

"He who is in love is a slave. He who is loved is the master," spoke a deep, insidious voice.

"Who said that? Where are you? What kind of joke is this? Where am I? Well, dammit, answer me!" I insisted.

"I, Possession, do not have to answer anyone," the disembodied voice reverberated all around me.

"Dammit, you had better start by answering me or—"

"Or what? I, Possession, possessor of the Sandpipers and proprietor of the Unconscious Power, will ask and thou shalt answer," a streak of lightning flashed pass me and thunder roared as he spoke.

"Look. Where am I, and where are you?" I asked cautiously.

"Ha, ha, ha, you are here. I am beside you, under you, in front of you, behind you, above you, and all around you." There was silence for a moment, then, "Who are you, and where are you from?"

"My name is Michael Anthony and I'm from Richmond, which is a city in the state of Virginia, which is located in the United States of America, which is a part of—"

"Silence!"

"I was only trying to be—"

"*Silence*! I say."

Thunder roared, but then there was a gentler, more conciliatory tone. "Is that not the Ring of Pisces upon your finger?" Just then a light from seemingly nowhere shone upon my finger, making the ring visible. I could clearly see the sign of Pisces deeply engraved in a primitive-looking platinum ring.

"What do you mean the ring of Pisces? It's my ring, and I bought it at a head shop in California."

"Liar!" another streak of lightning flashed past me and thunder roared as he spoke. "Now I know why you have come to the Land of the Sandpipers. Pisces gave you the ring and sent you here from the Third Stone from the Yellow Sun to kill me. Ha, ha, you shall not succeed, for I shall banish you to the havoc of the Blue Sun, where you shall be slain by Savoy, the keeper of the Blue Sun. Ha, ha, ha!"

Before I knew it, I found myself in a very hot cavern of blue. All along the walls were blue flames. I was startled to find a very beautiful and very nude woman of blue standing about five feet behind me. Her hair was icy blue, and it was moving around wildly as if it was alive or the wind was blowing. But it couldn't have been the wind because there was no wind. All she did was stand there and look me over for a minute. I tried to communicate with her, but she did not say a word.

Suddenly her hair began to grow longer, moving toward me, all the while swaying in midair. I was mesmerized by her. It was enchanting to watch her hair as it wrapped itself around me and began to pull me toward her. I had been pulled half way to her when she smiled and exposed her long, sharp teeth and that was when I broke free of the trance and began to try to free myself. It seemed hopeless, for her hair had a death grip on me. I was only about two feet from her when I felt the weight of something in my hand. It was a silvery double-edged sword. I instinctively swung the sword and cut off her head, but it did nothing to aid my being free, for the hair was still pulling me toward the head which was now on the ground and was still very much alive. I swung a second time at the hair, cutting myself free, but only for a moment for the hair grew at a faster rate than before. It wrapped itself around my ankles, causing me to fall. In doing so, I dropped the sword, but fortunately, it fell with the tip of the blade landing in her face. The hair ceased growing and turned to ashes. A moment later, I found myself back in darkness, and before I could say, "Phew!" a light shone on my finger and I saw the ring disappear.

"Ha, ha, ha, now what can you do without your ring? I would kill you, but I can use you. For you resemble the White People of So-Lo. The White People and the Black People live together in So-Lo but in hatred of one another. I long to possess them, but Kush, the first son of Summer, watches over them—the fool. I will have you destroy Kush."

"Never, slick! You aren't making me kill anyone. That just isn't my bag," I yelled defiantly.

The devious voice of Possession spoke, "I have not the power to make you destroy, but I know your weaknesses, and it won't be long before you will beg me to do as I bid. Ha, ha, ha!"

CHAPTER III

Anita Aguilar

I suddenly found myself standing beside a diamond-shaped bed in the middle of a sparsely decorated room. Light streamed into the room through a beautiful stained glass window opposite the bed. Upon closer examination, I saw that the stained glass window was a holographic projection. There were no windows. On the bed, asleep under red silk covers, was the girl I had saved earlier. Her smooth white complexion, glistening black hair, and Hispanic facial features made her alluring. I thought to myself, *Who is she? Could she be a goddess or something? I wish she were awake.*

As I examined the room, I noticed that the room and everything in it was the same color: red. I then realized that I was hungry. I walked out in search of food. While searching, I noticed that each room was a different shape and color, and everything in each room was the same design and color, but there were no windows or a door leading to the outside. Some of the things in the house, if you want to call it that, were so modern that I didn't know what they were. Well, I guess my search lasted about five minutes before I gave up and in frustration sat my butt in a round, glass chair in the room next to the bedroom. The room itself was white and round. The chair was hollow, padded, fur-lined, and suspended in midair without visible supports.

I had begun to relax when I heard a scream from the bedroom. I ran in to see what was wrong. The girl was turning wildly from side to side as if she were trying to free herself from something. I grabbed her arms and said, "Wake up! Wake up!" She stopped and opened her eyes and looked at me in fear. "It's all a dream. Just a bad dream," I assured her.

Still with a look of fear in her eyes, she whispered, "Who are you? How did you get in here? What are you going to do to me? Where did you—"

"Wait a minute now," I said with a smile. "Just hold on. One question at a time. Now to start with, my name is Michael Anthony and I'm not going to harm you. As for how I got here, well, I don't know. I was hoping you could answer that. Now it's…"

Just then, I noticed that she had a blank look on her face, as if she were having an epileptic seizure. After a few minutes of silence, she looked at me with knowing eyes and said, "I do not fear you because Mandala has assured me that you speak the truth. She also told me that you saved me from the eagle. Oh, she wants you to know that your ring does not possess magical powers, but it was she who provided you with the weapons. Tell me, what did she mean about the ring and the weapons?"

"Well, this Possession person thinks I was sent here by Pisces to destroy him. You see, my ring has the astrological sign I was born under, Pisces, engraved on it. And every time I've gotten into a jam, something magical has happened, such as a weapon would appear from nowhere. Now, how about you explain. Who is Mandala, what is your name, where are you from, why are you here, and where is there something to eat? I'm starving!"

Her smile expressed kindness as she spoke, "If you will leave while I put something on, I will get us both something to eat, and while we eat, we can talk and explain things to each other. Oh, by the way, my name is Anita Aguilar."

CHAPTER IV

Dinner

"Anita? It's a deal!" I said while getting off the bed.

As I walked out of the room, she asked, "Would you like to wash up and put on some other clothes? It must be kind of cool with just those swimming trunks on."

I stopped and nodded my approval. Saying nothing, she reached down beside the bed and picked up a small black box with different colored buttons on it. She pressed one of the buttons, and the wall to the left of the bed disappeared, revealing a large bathing pool.

"Now that's what I call service," I said cheerfully.

Wearing a blue knitted turtleneck jumpsuit and a pair of light-blue suede shoes, I emerged from the bedroom to find her sitting on a round glass sofa wearing a white silk Roman toga and a sweet, innocent smile on her face. From the moment I walked in and saw her sitting there smiling at me, I felt strange all over. The only time I felt that way was when I was with Brenda. "Come on, don't just stand there. Dinner is served."

I walked over and sat down beside her. In front of us, on the round glass table, were two glasses of water and two white pills. I looked at her and asked, "Where?"

"Where, what?"

"Where is dinner?"

"Michael, the pills are dinner. So eat!"

After reluctantly taking the pill, I said, "I would have preferred something I could have put my teeth into."

"Well, I would have given you solid food, but this is all Possession gives me to eat."

"Okay. How about answering my questions now."

"Well, I told you my name, and I'm from El Campo, Texas, and—"

"Wait a minute, Texas as in America? On earth?"

"Yes. Michael, are you from—"

I interrupted, "Virginia, Richmond. Virginia, on earth."

We both asked at the same time, "What are you doing here?"

"Look, why don't you just tell me your story first and I'll tell you mine," I said intently.

"Okay!" She settled into a more comfortable position on the sofa as she began to talk. "Well, I was going to get married, but at the last moment, I decided that marriage wasn't for me. Everyone was very angry with me, so I ran away from home. I had just gotten a job and an apartment in Corpus Christi when one night, while I was sleeping, a voice spoke to me. I awakened to find Mandala, the goddess of love. She was homely looking. My first reaction was to call the police, but her voice had a calming effect on me, so I listened. She told me she would introduce me to love. Well, she transported me to all these different places, and I do mean different, and I met many different people. I guess that's what you call some of them. Anyway, something wrong happened and I found myself here and Possession claimed me. There was nothing Mandala could do to get me away from him."

"Well, what was with the eagle?" I asked.

"Possession takes me for a toy." She shuddered a bit and said, "Michael, let's talk about something else, please? It's your turn. Why don't you tell me what you are doing here or at least how you got here?"

After explaining my story, I asked, "Is there a door to this crib?"

"Yes. I can open it with the black box. But why?" Fear began to creep across her face.

"Look, there has got to be a better place than this." I rose from sofa abruptly and extended my hand toward her, "Come on!"

She asked, "What are you going to do?"

"We're leaving this place!" I was emphatic.

Fearfully, she exclaimed, "No, Michael, there is no escape. I have tried many times before."

"If you won't come with me, I'll go by myself. Are you coming?"

Sadly, she replied, "No." For some odd reason, I began to feel hurt and disappointed, but I had to leave.

CHAPTER V

I Luv U

I had stepped no more than two feet beyond the door when two Sandpipers appeared from nowhere. The only direction away from the house was toward these two zombies, for there was a twenty-foot-high wall of sand on both sides of me. Walking slowly toward them, I said, "Well, friends, it's been nice, but I've got to go."

Just then, one of them pushed me back toward the door and the other extended his arm and pointed one finger out as if to say, "Go back inside!"

Starting out again in their direction, I said, "Yeah, slick, I understand what you mean, but I just can't stay."

Again when I came within their reach, I was pushed back toward the door. I started toward them a third time, but when I was within their reach, I threw a mean side kick to the stomach of one of them, but my foot went through him. I withdrew my foot and stood there in disbelief when the other one grabbed me and threw me hard to the ground. I got up in a rage and began to fight, but each punch I threw had no effect on them. It was as if they had no substance. I was thrown to the ground again and again. I finally got smart. I dove right through their bodies. But when I landed, I found myself on the floor of the house with Anita kneeling beside me. Then I heard the menacing, disembodied voice of Possession. "Ha, ha, ha, you gave a very good account of yourself, but a word to the wise is sufficient. You cannot leave until I release you. Ha, ha, ha!"

I looked at Anita and asked, "Is this real?"

"Michael, I know how you feel, but all you can do is stay here until something happens."

"Well, let's see what happens tonight. I'll take the sofa and you can take the bedroom."

She brought me some blankets to sleep under and returned to her bedroom after wishing me a pleasant night. The night was peaceful until I found myself walking down a dark, cold corridor. Suddenly I felt someone pat me on the back. To my surprise, it was Anita. She seemed as though she had fallen down a chimney. She was full of soot and blood was streaming down the right side of her face onto her shoulder. She wore a white slip which had been torn such that her right breast was visible. She stared at me with a blank look on her face; she was in shock. I shook her and asked, "What the hell happened to you?" She didn't speak. I screamed at her, "Anita, say something! Say something!"

"Michael! Wake up, Michael! Michael, wake up!"

I opened my eyes and found Anita sitting beside me and shaking my shoulders. I sat up abruptly, caressed her cheeks lovingly and kissed her passionately. After I kissed her, she just sat there gawking at me for a moment. I rather clumsily said, "Eh, look I, eh, don't know what came over me, but eh, I apologize for eh…"

"Don't apologize please. It was rather nice."

I kissed her again. We looked at each other for a minute afterward, and then I confessed, "I love you!"

With a look of amazement on her face, she stood up and said, "You're crazy."

"Please don't say that," I pleaded.

"No! I don't mean crazy, crazy, but different, unique. Oh, Michael, how can you say that you love me when you don't even know me?"

"I know me and love is what I feel. Believe me, 'Nita, *I love you!*"

She sat down beside me once again and asked, "Are you sure?"

"Dammit, I told you how I feel."

"You're serious!" she exclaimed

"You're damn right. *I love you!*" I grabbed her. We kissed lovingly and passionately.

CHAPTER VI

The Journey Across Moon Country

The following morning, I was awakened by a kiss. When I opened my eyes, she said with an endearing look in her eyes, "I love you!" After I kissed her, she said smiling, "You're a nut, but I love you."

Then she picked up a white fluffy pillow and hit me with it, which led into a pillow fight that ended in her bedroom and our making passionate love again. I was on my hands and knees looking down upon her when I said, "I wish we were somewhere else. Free to enjoy life and love."

She reached up, pulled me toward her, and kissed me tenderly. When we came out of the kiss, I opened my eyes to find green grass and trees all around us and we were wearing clothes. We looked at each other baffled. The bed and the house were gone. She asked, "Is this all a dream?"

"No! At least I don't think so because we both wouldn't have the same dream," I replied. But then I asked, "Could this be Mandala's work?"

"No, Mandala does not have the power to take us away from Possession."

I looked around again and said softly, "I know this place."

"What did you say?" she asked.

"I said I know this place!"

I turned my head quickly back to her and asked with a smile, "'Nita, do you know where we are?"

Before she could answer, I said, "Maymont Park! We're somewhere in Maymont Park, which means we are on earth. Maymont Park is in Richmond, Virginia."

Just then, I began to feel strange. But I didn't care; we were back on earth. It wasn't long before we were loving and enjoying ourselves. Each day, there was something different to do and in a different place—from grooving on cool jazz by famous musicians at the Jazz Festival at Hampton Institute to riding over sand dunes in a dune buggy in Corpus Christi, Texas. And each day, I loved her more and more.

Suddenly, it all disappeared and I found myself in darkness listening to the insidious voice of Possession, "He who is in love is a slave. He who is loved is the master. Ha, ha, ha, your fun is over. Now you will do as I bid, for you are in love and I possess your loved one. Love is your vice. Ha, ha, ha."

"If I don't do what you want, what happens?"

"Anita will die. But if you do as I bid, she will live. Choose!"

I cried out in anger, "Where is she?"

"She is where no one can find her—not even Mandala knows. You may see her when you come back and I have possession of the Black People and White People of So-Lo. *Choose*!" Bright white lightning flashed and thunder roared.

"Okay, slick, you win. Let's hurry and get this over with," I said bitterly. I loved her and I didn't want her harmed.

"You must travel over the Moon Country to get to So-Lo. You start as soon as you get the ring of Pisces."

Suddenly, a light shone upon my finger and the ring appeared. Before I knew what had happened, I faced miles and miles of sand and rock and mountains.

Depressed and angry with myself, I started on my journey across the Moon Country. I had only traveled a mile when I heard a female's voice call my name. I whipped around, but she was nowhere to be found. I called out in anger, "All right, stop playing games. Who are you, and what do you want?"

"Michael, I am Mandala and I called your name and said nothing afterward to see if my brother, Possession, was around. I came to give you mental strength. Anita loves you and she needs you just as much as you need her. No matter what happens, she always will love you."

I just stood there for a moment then said with great determination, "We will make it, 'Nita. We will make it."

CHAPTER VII

So-Lo

The journey through the Moon Country was hot and arduous. It took three long days and two nights. On the third day, I saw an enormous blue-gray stone statue of an eye. In the center of the eye, there was nothing but a deep darkness. On the other side of the eye, there was grass and trees and real animals that seemed friendly, but for some reason, they did not seem interested in wandering into Moon Country. After crossing over to the land of grass, trees, and animals, two things happened. I noticed the hole in the center of the eye was not black with darkness, but instead, one could see the setting of the blue sun. It was then that I realized that Possession had no more power over me except that he possessed Anita. I also realized that I was very, very hungry, but I continued on until I fell to the ground in exhaustion.

When morning came, I started out again in search of food and So-Lo, in that order. It wasn't long before I came across a farmhouse which was completely white. Even the iron fence around it was white. I walked up the steps and knocked on the door, hoping that someone would answer.

When the door opened, I was more than surprised to find a little black boy with a white water pistol in his hand. All I could do was just look at him. For a minute he did the same, then he ran away screaming, "Mama, Daddy, there's a Black People that looks like a White People at the door."

Minutes later, there was a black man and woman standing at the door staring at me, and the little boy was peeping at me from behind the woman's pink dress. I asked to come in, but they emphatically responded in unison with, "*No!*"

A minute later, the gentleman spoke to his wife and said, "He doesn't look like a White Man, but he doesn't look like a Black Man either."

"Maybe he's a cross between Black and White," she said.

I was getting hungrier by the minute, so in frustration I shouted, "Black or White, please tell me how to get to So-Lo and give me something to eat."

"Well, whatever he is, he certainly isn't White," the man said to his wife.

And with that, the door was slammed shut in my face. Depressed, angry, and hungry, I turned and faced the gate through which I had come when the little boy opened the door and said, "The city is just over the hill," and quickly slammed the door.

I looked around and saw a large, grassy hill with a smattering of Indian paintbrush and Texas bluebonnet flowers just behind the house and started out toward it. After crossing it, I saw the city of So-Lo. It resembled a western town of olden days like in the movies. While walking down the main street, which was the only street, I noticed that on one side of the street, everything was white and the people were African and on the other side of the street everything was black and the people were Caucasian. On both sides of the street, the buildings were the same. I further noticed that the people never crossed from one side of the street to the other. After walking for a little while, everyone stopped and stared at me. After a minute had passed, someone from the White side asked, "What is he, Black or White?"

Then someone on the other side shouted, "He's got White People's hair."

"Yeah, but his skin isn't as dark as ours, and then again, it isn't as light as theirs. What the hell is he?"

"He must be a spy for the Black People," a woman shouted loudly. Then a stone hit me on my right arm and a voice loudly cried out, "Kill!"

Stones began to fly from one side of the street to the other. People were screaming foul words at one another and children were crying. Chaos became the order of the day.

Suddenly, the sky seemed to open and a bright light shone down upon me, and I found myself in a place that was brightly lit. I looked around behind me to find a triangular cloud that continually changed into all the colors of a rainbow. I looked at it in puzzlement when a calm, deep, masculine voice spoke to me.

"I am the one you seek, Michael. I am Kush. There is no need to explain. I know what has happened and why you have sought me."

"Well, that's heavy. You know everything, yet you sit by and ignore what happens to everyone and anyone!"

"Yes, but let me explain. You see, my purpose is not to get involved in the affairs of others. I am to merely hand down to them my knowledge and let them learn what they will, when they will. Mr. Woodruff explained something similar to you long ago. Am I not right?"

"Well, yeah, but what about Possession?"

"Possession has gone too far now and my father, Summer, agrees with me that Possession must be put away."

"Okay, that's cool, but what about 'Nita. He has her."

"Do not worry, she will be released. My father and I ask that you put Possession away. You see, I cannot harm another and my father cannot do any harm to anyone unless someone does harm to one of the family. This is why Possession was wise to choose someone else to do his bidding."

"Great, now tell me how I am going to do this," I said in disbelief.

"You will be able to imprison Possession in the Glass Onion by merely exposing him to it. He will not be able to escape." Suddenly, there floating in the air before me appeared the Glass Onion. "Take it with you and do not let Possession know you have it until he surrounds you. After you have put him away and Anita is with you, go to the Eye, the stone statue you passed by on your why here. Jump into the center of the darkness and you will leave this place. You must go now. The Crimson Shell will transport you."

That very instant, I found myself standing in a large crimson seashell over Moon Country. The shell took me to the Land of the Sandpipers. It landed in front of this huge igloo made of sand. I got out and walked in to find that the inside resembled a church. All the Sandpipers were there. Some seemed to be listening to a sermon given by Possession, who was in a pulpit that rose high into the ceiling. The others were sleeping. I began to walk toward the pulpit when suddenly, I found myself in darkness and Possession spoke.

"So I see you have returned alive. I sense you did not complete your mission, or you would have destroyed both Kush and Summer, which is not possible. Not even Pisces has the power to do that. So why are you back?"

"It's very simple, slick. I've got something to show you." At that moment, I took my hand with the Glass Onion in it out of my pocket to show it to him.

CHAPTER VIII

The Eye

The next moment, I found myself standing in the Crimson Shell with Anita beside me and the Glass Onion floating upward out of my hand. Anita grabbed me and began to cry. I was overjoyed to see that she had been returned to me. I told the shell to proceed to the Eye. As we proceeded toward the Eye, I filled her in on what had taken place.

It wasn't long before we reached the Eye. When we arrived, the shell positioned itself at the center of the Darkness. I turned to Anita and said, "This is it! It's now or never." I grabbed her hand tightly, and we jumped into the darkness together. It was only moments before we were engulfed in a whirlpool of multicolored lights and piercing shrill sounds.

"We made it!" I shouted.

Then I realized that I couldn't feel her hand, the hand of the woman I was so in love with. I looked around for her, but she was nowhere to be found. Tears immediately came to my eyes.

"Alone! Once again, I'm alone, no one. Funny, but I always seem to end up alone. Not a soul to love me, while I go from place to place. I love her! Now she's gone. *Anita!*"

"Michael!" a deep husky voice spoke. "I am OM—"

"You're supposed to be dead," I interrupted.

"I made you think that because it was the only way you could understand at the time, but enough of that. I speak because there are two things you must understand. First, your journey will never come to an end. The reason is yours to figure out. I am confident you can. Second, Anita still loves you. She has not left you because she wants to but because she has a life to live and things to find out about herself just as you, and she can do this best without you. The days that you two were together are over for now. When you two jumped, you both went back to living your separate lives. But your lives may cross again. So do as Young Girl Sunday Blues said. Live!"

The voice of OM faded, and I said to myself with tears in my eyes, "Alone and staring at the unseen. Alone!"

Part III
Alone

Fly blue sky, voices keep calling
Bidding me welcome, why maiden land's
Luring me closer, forbidden land

And as I'm standing closer
Those natives step beyond

Release the mortal patterns
My mind I post beyond

Spinning in circles, miracles happen
As lower life shows me into my doom
Spirit will stricken, the end will come soon

This is termination
The outcome of your life

—Iron Butterfly, "Termination"

CHAPTER I

Vietnam

The stars were still shining brightly above the scattered clouds. It would only be a matter of time before the sun would begin to rise and shine bright over Vietnam once more. The moon hadn't shown its face much that night, which made it a bit hazardous for the convoy of US Marine Corps tractor trailers (TTs) on their motor march to a nearby airstrip where the Marines of the Ninth MAB, the Third BN FMF, and part of FCSG—Bravo Company of the Third. Marines would be picked up by planes to be taken to Da Nang and from there to Okinawa. I was in a TT in about the middle of the convoy, and I was standing up front just behind the cab of the truck thinking about the future to come back in the world.

Just about everyone was sacked out in the trailer except for myself and a few others. I was deep in thought when someone placed their hand on the back of the ALICE pack I was wearing and said in a very friendly voice, "Well, what da ya say there, Corporal Anthony?"

I didn't turn around to see who it was because I knew it was Sergeant Duran. He was the only one that would ever ask me that question. Sergeant Duran was five feet and five inches tall, thirty-nine years old, and balding on top. He was a pretty cool white dude who taught me a great deal during my stay in Vietnam. He came along side me and asked, "Well, Corporal, how does it feel to finally be leaving Dong Ha and going back to the world?"

"Sergeant Duran, you know exactly how I feel." I wore a big smile on my face.

As I listened to myself talk, I began to realize that I had just jumped into the center of the Eye, and only moments ago, I was falling through a whirlpool of colorful lights and sounds. How and why was I in the past? This had already happened a year or so ago. It was then that I remembered that in a matter of minutes, the convoy would be ambushed by a very large contingent of the North Vietnamese Army and Viet Cong, but for some reason, I could only bring myself to talk about all the beautiful love affairs that I was going to have when I got to Okie—Okinawa, the rock, the world.

Suddenly, before I could realize what was happening, the lead truck blew up and three flares went up lighting the entire area. Almost instantly, we were hit from all directions by automatic and semi-automatic fire. Blood poured from the bodies of sleeping marines. I saw one marine jump up to fight the enemy only to have his face blown off by a fifty caliber that entered from the back of his head. He never had an opportunity to point his riffle in the direction of the enemy. I was scared shitless!

Then the truck in front of us burst into flames, killing almost everyone on board; body parts went everywhere. Sergeant Duran and I leapt from the truck we were in and took cover. As soon as I hit the ground, I quickly scurried under the truck and began firing my M16 into the surrounding bushes. I could see that Sergeant Duran was in trouble as I fired at the unseen enemy. Duran was about fifty feet away from me and bleeding badly. He was hit in the legs and he couldn't move, but he kept firing even though he couldn't see his assailants. I crawled from under the truck and ran toward him, while firing my weapon in all directions. I had gotten no more than a few feet away from the truck when it went up in flames, killing every Marine very near it. When I reached Sergeant Duran, he looked at me and said, "Well, what da ya say there, Corporal Anthony?"

"Yeah, dig it, Sergeant. What are you trying to do, get killed?"

I grabbed him and started to make my way toward a hole that had been made by a mine sometime earlier. I had moved no more than five feet when I stepped on a mine. I didn't even have enough time to see my life flash before me.

But wait, that wasn't supposed to happen, I thought to myself. "Duran and I lived through that ambush. At least that's my recollection. How could the past have been changed and why? What the hell was going on?"

CHAPTER II

The Garden of Eden

Suddenly I found myself in a beautiful garden. It looked much the way I pictured the Garden of Eden—lush, green, and full of trees, bushes, and flowers of every description.

"Am I dead?" I asked myself aloud as I looked around. "Is this heaven?"

"No! I just thought it would be a pleasant place for us to meet," a very calm voice said.

I turned around quickly to see who had spoken, but all that I saw was a bush aflame in bright orange, red, and yellow. I was fascinated by it. Not because of the biblical reference but because there was no smoke nor heat being emitted from the burning bush. It reminded me of a politician by the same name: all show, no go. "You have very good reflexes, Michael."

"Thank you for the compliment, but would you mind telling me where you are or who you are or both?" I continued to look around for my host.

"Look in front of you, Michael."

"Well, I'll be damned. I'm in heaven and God is talking to me through a burning bush just like he did to that dude, what's his name."

"It was Moses, but this is not heaven and I am not that fictitious character in the Bible named God," the voice from the flame said in anger.

"I am Ontos, the god of war. Possession was my brother and you must pay for what you did to him." The voice was more reserved.

"Well, no shit. And I suppose you are the one who changed my past?"

"I didn't change your past. I brought you to an alternate dimension or universe. It was the only way I could capture your ass to make you pay."

"How am I supposed to pay? What are you going to do, burn me at the stake or something?" I said sarcastically.

"You are going to be my plaything, my bitch. My friends, Shiva, the god of destruction, and Kala, the god of death, have helped me devise an interesting game."

"Well, what if I don't want to play?"

"You have no choice, but you'd stand a chance of living if you play the game."

"How?" A gentle breeze caressed my face and the sweet smell of lilac fondled my nostrils.

"You will fight another, who we feel is worthy of battle with you. The two of you will fight to the death. If you kill him, you will live, but if he kills you, he will live. If you do not accept the fight, death is assured." I could almost hear him smile.

"Look, can't we talk this over? I mean, besides your brother had it coming to him."

"You will be transported by a trapezohedron crystal to a place that is similar to earth."

CHAPTER III

The Game Begins

Before I could say another word, I found myself lying on my back inside a trapezohedron crystal, traveling through the Divine Attribute at a fantastic speed. Suddenly, I found myself under a rocky overhang. A minute later, the crystal disappeared, enabling me to move again.

I got to my feet slowly. As I did, I noticed that I was nude and my head was bald. After a minute or so, I began to look around for my opponent. While searching, I noticed that the environment resembled the Great Western Plateau of Australia—deep red sand and rock. The vegetation was mostly drought-resistant shrub. As I walked around, I realized that I was standing atop a cliff, which was a part of a series of unbroken cliffs that stretched for miles.

As I looked around further, I saw a very strange sight. About fifty feet to the left of me in the middle of nowhere was a yew tree. While walking toward it, I heard a peculiar crackling sound. I turned around to see what it was and spied a second crystal dissipating and depositing a human form under the same rocky overhang I had found myself under. It was about ten feet away. I thought maybe if I went over, I could come to terms with my opponent—if it was my opponent.

When I reached him, I was astonished to find that I was staring at myself, or what appeared to be a duplicate of me—bald head and all. The only physical difference was that it had no penis. I was so shocked all I could do was stand there gawking with my mouth wide open and my eyes as big as saucers.

Suddenly the other me jumped to his feet and grabbed me by the shoulders with a vice-like grip and slung me several feet away. I just laid on the ground for about a minute or so to see if I had any broken bones. Luckily, there were none, but there were a few cuts and bruises and I ached all over. Out of the corner of my eye, I saw him approaching, and on his face was a fierce look that said, "Kill!"

I began to get to my knees slowly as if I were really hurting and I was. I waited until he was at arm's reach, then leaped toward him head first, hitting him in the stomach and causing him to fall backward. When he hit the ground, I felt him grab my waist and before I could say, "Shit!" I was making like a bird, only to land face first in the dirt.

This time I got to my feet as quickly as possible and got into the nekoashi-dachi or cat stance position and waited for him to come to me. When he arrived, I unleashed the yoko geri kekomi (high side) kick, which was quickly followed by a mae tobi geri (front) kick and a choku zuki (straight) punch to the head, which caused him to back off but not much.

He came back for more, and this time, he was blocking every punch and kick I threw at him. And I also noticed that he was developing greater speed with his blocks. In fact, it wasn't long before I was the one trying to block his kicks and punches. After receiving a few painful punches, I backed off but only to literally find myself between a rock and a hard place. My back was up against a rock wall. As he slowly approached, I picked up a boulder and threw it at him. He caught it and threw it back. I ducked just in time and took off running.

I managed to get away from him and hide long enough to rest and figure out what the hell was happening and what to do next. But the rest didn't last long. I just happened to look up when I saw him. There he was standing above me on a rock ledge. He jumped down on top of me, but I managed to get a punch in to the head that stunned him long enough for me to get away again. This time I ran and ran until I couldn't run any longer. Out of breath, I fell to my knees and blacked out.

CHAPTER IV

I Kill Me

I woke up to find the sun setting and a red desert scorpion no more than inches from my right arm, bringing its tail and poisonous stinger into striking position. I stayed very still, and with my left hand, picked up a rock and swiftly crushed the thing. I spent that night in a cave, and the following morning, I began to fashion a crude knife out of stone found in the cave.

The day was half over and I was half finished with my knife when I saw him in the distance. I got behind a large boulder just outside the cave and waited. He approached the cave with caution and was about to enter when I leaped toward him from my hiding place and at the same time gave a frightening scream. He whipped around with fantastic speed and knocked my weapon from my hand and grabbed me by the throat with his left hand and proceeded to choke the life out of me.

By instinct, I kneed him in the groin area. He let me go and screamed in pain. I kicked him again in the same area and the same thing happened, only he screamed louder. I went in for another, but this time he blocked it and hit me with a hard right to my jaw. I stumbled and fell over a rock. He started to come in for the kill with my knife in his hand, but I kicked with both feet to his face. He backed off long and far enough that I could get to my feet under me and run away to live and fight another day. I lost him in the distance and sat down to think. "I know his weak point. How can I use it to my advantage?" I said to myself.

"Michael, have a care!" I jumped to my feet thinking that it was him, but shortly afterward, I realized it was Mandala. I frantically looked about for her but saw no one. Angrily I shouted, "Fuck it! Where are you?"

"Michael, have a care," her mellifluous voice was calming.

"I'm being chased around by some nude character who looks like me. I hurt all over, I'm tired, sick, and hungry. And you, wherever you are, tell me to have a care. Wow!"

"Michael, I am here in your mind. I've come to warn you of the danger you are in."

"Well, you're too goddamn late. I know already!" I said exasperatedly.

"Be quiet and listen. You don't have much time. The creature that is after you is, in large part, you. It can only be killed by you with one powerful blow to his groin. If you win the fight, you will live, but you will forever be a slave to Ontos, Shiva, and Kala in this place."

"And if I don't win?"

"If you don't win, you will die, but that part of you that is him will be a slave to them forever. Whether you win or lose, in either case, you will die or be a slave forever as yourself or your opponent. As it stands, you are fighting yourself."

"Well, how do I get out of this fix?"

"You must both kill each other with your deaths occurring at almost the same time. But remember, you are in an alternate dimension. Anything can happen afterward. I must go now. Have a care."

I sat down and said, "Now how can we both kill each other at the same time?" I thought for a moment and it hit me, the solution.

Without wasting any time, I went off in search of him. It didn't take long to find him. I began to harass him, and at the same time, I was moving in the direction of the cliffs.

It wasn't long before I found myself standing on the edge of the cliffs with him facing me. He stopped a few feet in front of me, looking over the situation. I peeped over my right shoulder to see what it looked like below. There was a straight drop down to the water at the bottom with huge, dark, jagged rocks jutting upward from the water's edge. I turned and looked at him and said, "Slick, one of these days you're going to thank me."

I carefully picked up a medium-sized purple rock and threw it at him. It hit him in the groin, and he screamed and charged at me with the knife I made. When we made contact, we clung to each other, and as he drove the knife deep into my weary body, I hit him as hard as I could in the groin. While he was distracted by his pain, I pulled the knife from my chest, and plunged it into his groin. With our last dying breaths, we both fell over the edge into oblivion.

Part IV

The First Snow of Summer After A Long, Hot Winter: So the Gods Made Love

When I said, "You have grown thin,"
She came and clung to me.
"Your clothes are bedraggled," I said,
And she hung down her head.
When I said, "I can hardly see you,"
Her big breasts heaved and she wept.
When I embraced her,
She was troubled with indescribable love,
And in an instant, the doe-eyed girl
Was completely merged in my heart.

—Marula by Jambimuttu and G. V. Vaiclya,
"Meeting After Separation"

CHAPTER I

Excuse Me

"Excuse me, but would you gentlemen like a cocktail?" A very interesting and pleasant female voice asked, which was followed by, "No, thank you!"

"Huh. I beg your pardon, but did you ask something?" I asked at the same time turning my head in her direction and blinking my eyes two or three times, trying to get a clear focus of to whom I was speaking.

"Eh, sir, I asked if you gentlemen were interested in a cocktail?" she said. By this time, my visual perception of her was clear, and I could see that she was an airline stewardess. I could also see that she was tall but well-proportioned, and she had blue eyes and platinum blond hair. "Well, sir, do you want a cocktail?" she asked, this time expressing that her time was very important.

"Huh, no, thank you. I don't drink. Eh, by the way are we onboard a jet airliner?"

"Yes, we are sir," she said looking at me in a strange manner.

"Eh, how did I get on board?" I asked.

"Well, I guess you walked on, sir."

"Thank you, miss. You may leave us now. It seems as though my friend is having a joke on you," said the Caucasian gentleman sitting beside me on my left. He was somewhat heavy with green eyes, a moustache, and a Van Dyke.

The stewardess left in a huff as I turned to him and said angrily, "Hey, you're a pretty righteous dude, but I don't feel you had the right to cut in like that and send her away. She wasn't talking to you, and I'd also like to know what your bag is, calling me your friend?"

"Look, Mr. Cole—"

"Wait a minute, how about starting over by calling me by my name. Anthony, not Cole."

"Look, Cole, I don't know what your game is, but if you had not killed Anthony, I'd have a bit more respect for you as a human being, but I don't. So as long as you are in my custody, you will do as I say until we get to Washington, DC."

"Hey, eh, I know you didn't say that I killed Michael Anthony because if you did you're wrong. I'm Michael Anthony, so you must be mixed up."

He grabbed my collar with both hands. As he collared me, I was shocked to see that my left wrist was handcuffed to his right wrist. A few seconds later, everyone in the coach of the plane was trying to see what was going on when the guy beside him talked him into cooling it. I wanted to ask this cat his name, but I decided it would be best to keep my mouth shut. I took a deep breath and pulled out a handkerchief from the suit I didn't know I was wearing until then. After using the handkerchief to wipe my forehead, I felt the top of my head to see if I was bald, but oddly enough, I had a full head of hair. I sat back in my seat and began to try and figure out what was going on.

Okay, Mike, I thought to myself, *from the way things appear, you're on earth, and the guy beside you thinks you're some dude named Cole. Not only that but this cat's taking you to Washington because he says you killed yourself. More than likely, this is some sort of wild hallucination or weird nightmare. If you get some sleep, everything will be back to normal when you wake up. Right? Right!* I settled back to get some shut eye.

CHAPTER II

Corpus Christi

I slept for about an hour or more before I was awakened by the head stewardess's voice over the public address system. "We are now preparing to land at Corpus Christi International Airport in Corpus Christi, Texas. Please fasten your seatbelts and put out all cigarettes. There will be an hour layover for mechanical adjustments and refueling. All passengers who will be leaving the plane permanently, we hope that you have had a pleasant trip and we welcome you to fly Trans World Airlines again. Thank you. Please do not unfasten your seatbelts until the plane has come to a complete stop."

The landing was exceptionally smooth and this bad dream was getting worse. When we entered the lobby of the airport, there were two grim looking men in navy-blue business suits to meet us. They were both somewhere around six feet tall and wore uncompromising expressions on their faces that matched their Ray-Ban aviator sunglasses.

"Well, it seems that when you get to Washington with Mr. Cole, there will be a reception committee of reporters waiting," so stated one of the blue suits in a very monotone way.

"Do you think we'll have any trouble?" my friend asked.

"Hey, guys, it would help me a hell of a lot if someone were to tell me what this is all about," I interrupted in a conciliatory tone.

"Is he kidding?" asked the other blue suit.

"Don't let him jive you. The great Mr. Les Cole has been playing stupid lately." My friend quickly changed the subject. "What about the four girls who worked with him?"

"The Vice Squad?"

"Yeah! Have they been found or at least identified?"

The suits looked at each other as if to decide who will speak and then one said, "*No*! The bureau is still looking into it."

As they talked, I surveyed my surroundings. They and their conversation were boring me to tears, and it was plain to me that I was not one of their favorite people. My survey caused me to notice a beautiful young woman walking toward one of the front exits of the lobby. As she walked through the exit, she dropped her handbag, and I was afforded a better view of her face. I soon realized that she was Anita. I was shocked. My emotions were heightened. I immediately began to focus my entire being on a way to set myself free of this stainless steel bracelet and the asshole on the other end, not to forget his friends. It was only a few seconds later that one of the blue suits fell to the floor with a loud thud; the other three looked on in wonder. Upon closer inspection, they found that their friend had been shot. I didn't waste time. I instinctively twisted my friend's right arm behind his back and began to apply upward pressure while simultaneously grabbing and squeezing his esophagus with my right hand. The other two quickly took aggressive postures when I shouted, "Back off or I'll kill him!"

They did as I commanded. I immediately reached under my friend's coat and relieved him of his Smith and Wesson .44 Magnum. Now with a gun in my possession, I anxiously shouted, "Okay, now, which one of you has the key to these goddamn cuffs!"

CHAPTER III

Escape

By this time, Anita had left the lobby, and I knew I would have to be quick to catch her. I repeated myself, this time pulling back the hammer on the revolver. It wasn't long before I was set free. I pushed my friend into the other two men and made them deposit their guns in a nearby trash can. As I ran toward the exit, I was fired upon by one of the airport security police. I quickly returned the fire, causing him to seek cover. My attention was so intensely focused on Anita that I didn't notice the chaos that surrounded me, nor did I notice that I had been shot in the arm. I darted out the exit door and onto the street. I looked for Anita, but when I spotted her, she was getting into an olive-green Pontiac GTO with a black vinyl top. I screamed her name again and again, but it was in vain for the car drove off. I ran after her thinking I had lost her for good now, when I noticed a dude preparing to mount his chopper. I stopped and shoved the very large, intimidating revolver in his face. "Sorry, slick, but I need your bike more than you. Dig it?"

Backing away slowly, he quickly agreed, "Yeah, man, just be cool."

"Peace to you too!" I drove off down the road in pursuit of my love. As the chopper roared down the road, I noticed that I was being pursued by my friends and the police. In the distance before me I could see the GTO, and I realized that it was heading straight for the bay area. It was not long before I found myself on Ocean Drive and heading south, not far behind the GTO. Soon after, I heard sirens and gunfire.

I accelerated to increase the distance between me and the pursuing cop cars. Try as I did, the police were still behind me and bullets continued zooming past. I knew I had to get some cars between me and them. The first car I passed, I faked it. I started to pass on the outside, but at the last minute, I cut back inside and passed him on the right. The cop car closest to me tried to follow suit, lost control, and spun off into the guardrail. While passing the second vehicle, I had the shit scared out of me. I was passing an eighteen-wheel Mack on the outside, but before I realized it, there was a twenty-two wheel Kenworth tractor trailer headed in my direction. It was too late to get back to safety, so I brought the chopper as close as I could to the Mack to avoid a head-on collision.

I was on the double yellow line when the Kenworth passed me by while blowing his horn like crazy. It was a tight squeeze. The cop car that followed me that time, careened through the guardrail on the left, and stopped on the beach while trying to avoid being hit by the Kenworth.

In all the excitement, I lost sight of the GTO. I lost Anita, but I hadn't lost my pursuers. The heat of a speeding bullet creasing the left side of my head brought me to that realization. The damn thing hurt like hell. I began to get dizzy, but I was determined not to give up. As I raced down the highway, I began to hear a new sound—a helicopter. I glanced over my shoulder and saw a black AH56A Cheyenne helicopter coming up the rear and kicking ass. The Cheyenne fired an air to ground missile and blew the shit out of two of the many police cars that were attempting to catch me. Minutes later, a police helicopter arrived on the scene, but it was no match for the Cheyenne. The police 'copter was blown to hell after receiving automatic fire from the Cheyenne.

I didn't know what to think, and when the Cheyenne came after me, evasion was on my mind. I was as helpless as a trout against an expert trout fisherman. The Cheyenne lowered a grappling cable, which was hooked the handle bar of the chopper, and carried me and the chopper away from the chaos and over the choppy bay. We were about a mile away from shore when I was overcome by dizziness, causing me to lose my grip and fall.

CHAPTER IV

Love Reclaimed

The fall wasn't painful, but the landing was hell. It was as if I had been thrown hard against a brick wall. The initial shock of hitting the cold, dense water was unpleasant to say the least. It took the breath out of me as I started to sink to the bottom of the bay. Every part of my being fought to stay alive. Upon reaching the surface, after having been submerged for what seemed like an eternity, I saw a yacht anchored just a short distance away. I began the swim of my life. The searing pain in my head had now spread throughout my entire body. I couldn't think. My vision was blurred. My lungs were burning and my guts were knotting up. I wanted to just lie down and sleep, but I continued to swim for what seemed like hours. I went for the gold but unconsciousness overwhelmed me, and I was swallowed up in the wet darkness.

"Ohhhh!" I said while falling back onto a fluffy pink pillow after trying to sit up. I rubbed my eyes with my right hand and felt a cloth bandage around my head. Upon further investigation, I found a second bandage around the upper part of my left arm. I waited a while, then tried again to get up from the bed. It didn't take much to make me realize just how weak I was. After much difficulty, I sat on the side of the bed and looked around the room in wonder while silently dealing with my pain. "Where the hell am I?" I asked myself.

It was a very small bedroom. In one corner of the room was a bureau and opposite it was a hand locker. Facing me was the only door in the room: a room without windows. I knew that I'd never get the answers to my many questions until I got off my ass, found my clothes, and walked through that door. I turned my head toward the bureau and said, "Well, if my clothes are here, they are in that bureau."

I began to wearily make my way to the bureau. When I finally reached the bureau, I found a newspaper lying on top. Since it was written in Spanish, about all I could make out on it was the year—1973.

"Well, it's nice to see that you're up," said a sweet female voice.

Startled, I turned around quickly to find—"Anita?" I asked. So dismayed, I totally forgot that I was wearing nothing but my skivvies.

She seemed somewhat shocked at first, but then she smiled and sweetly asked, "Since you seem to know my name, how about telling me yours?"

"'Nita, you haven't forgotten already, have you? You know me. Michael, Michael Anthony."

The expression on her face was that of consternation as she slowly walked over to me. She stopped about a foot in front of me and just looked at me for a moment. Before I could stop her, she slapped me twice with both hands and said angrily, "Go to hell!" She then turned and ran out of the room.

I didn't know what to do or think. I just stood there. My eyes began to fill with tears as one ran down my cheek. Dizzily, I returned to the bed and sat down. Subsequently, I put on a robe, which had been lying at the foot of the bed, and left the room in search of her. I didn't have to go far to find her nor to realize that I was onboard a boat. She was in the saloon sitting at the bar having a drink. As I approached her, I could see that there were tears in her eyes. I sat down beside her. She turned toward me and tried to slap me again, but this time I caught her hand and said, "I don't understand. Why?"

"Get the hell out of here and leave me alone!"

"What have I done? What's happening? Why?" I was perplexed.

"I don't know who you are, mister, but you had better get out of here."

"All right, I'll leave. But I want to know why you don't believe I'm Michael Anthony."

For the longest while, she said nothing. Then holding back tears, she said, "Michael Anthony was not, is not, and never will be real. He was just someone I made up in my mind. Now will you please go?"

I just looked at her. I was stunned. After a minute or so, I slowly rose from my seat and walked toward the door. When I reached the middle of the room, I stopped, turned, and said, "'Nita, I love you! Why the hell can't you see that I'm still me? Have I changed? Has it been that long? What the hell is wrong?" I walked over to her and firmly but tenderly held her face between the palms of my hands. "Anita, look at me. Touch me! Can't you see that it's me? The nut that fell in love with you? Don't you still love me?"

She looked at me and asked, "Where were you born?"

"Richmond! Richmond, Virginia."

"Where did we first meet?" she insisted.

"In the Land of the Sandpipers. What can I do to make you believe me?" I asked.

Then with her hands, she grabbed my right hand and held it away from her face so as to see it better. She was looking for the ring, the Ring of Pisces that I was wearing on my pinkie finger.

"You are Michael," she whispered with surprise.

I looked into her eyes for a moment and whispered, "I have missed you terribly. Believe me when I say I love you!"

"Oh, Michael. I love you! I can't believe it. Everyone told me I was crazy. My mother had me see a head doctor. I even thought she was going to have me committed. Michael, I thought you were playing me for a fool at first. I'm sorry I slapped you." She started to cry.

I caressed her and said, "Look, be cool and stop crying. You're messing up your eye makeup. Everything's all right now, baby. We're together again and that's all that matters. Now how about explaining things? What happened after you and I were separated?"

She calmed down and began. "I still don't quite know, but I found myself in bed at home. No one would believe my story. I kept trying to make them understand, but they just wouldn't. Well, my mother got sick of the whole thing and sent me to Dr. Oscar, a head doc. He more or less convinced me that I had been fantasizing. Now you show up out of nowhere. Mother told me that father had found you half-drowned, and he brought you onboard the yacht. When I saw you, I told myself that you were someone else, that you couldn't be Mike because you didn't exist. You had a fever and two bullet wounds and you kept calling my name. Mother was going to turn you over to the police, but I couldn't let that happen. I don't know why. So I begged her not to. I guess I had to be sure it wasn't you. She had my sister Mary, the nurse, care for your wounds and fever. Father took a picture of you to Frank Kellogg, a local detective and friend of the family, to find out more about you. And that's why you've been with us so long."

"Huh. How long has it been and where are we?"

"It's been about a week, and we are right off the coast of Panama. Everyone has gone inland except Jon and me. Jon is one of the crew."

"Why didn't you go too?" She answered my question by throwing her arms around my neck. We clung to each other for a moment in a tight embrace. I gently pushed her away from me and said, "We'll have plenty of time for this later. Right now, I want my clothes. Where are they?"

"Come on, I'll show you." We proceeded to return to the room I had just left.

CHAPTER V

Love and Happiness

When we arrived at the room, I sat on the bed while she retrieved my clothes from the hand locker. When she came to me with my clothes, I placed my hands around the small of her waist and pulled her onto the bed with me. Now was the time! It felt good to touch her again, to kiss her passionately again, to love her, and to be loved by her again. I felt a strong need inside me for her love and understanding. As we kissed, I told myself that I would never leave her again. I pulled away suddenly and asked, "How long has it been since we last made love?"

"Too long!"

"Well, I guess we'll just have to make up for lost time."

She smiled and said, "I don't see why not. No one will be back until tomorrow." That was all the incentive I needed.

When I awakened, I found 'Nita wheeling in breakfast on a cart.

"Hey, you nut. What are you doing out of bed?" I asked with a smile on my face.

"Well, you didn't look like you were going to get up and fix breakfast," she said smiling back at me. "And besides, I was hungry."

After eating, we went to the galley to wash the dishes when she suggested, "Hey, how about going skin diving?"

"That sounds great!"

The world beneath the yacht was beautiful, and being there with her made it that much more so. The fish moved in schools through the crystal blue water. There were giant sea turtles slowly maneuvering above the sea bottom. We explored this portion of the world beneath the sea right up to the shore where she removed her flippers, ran onto the beach, threw off her gear into the sand, and ran back to me smiling as I walked onto the beach after her. When she reached me, she threw her arms around me causing us to fall onto the white sand while our lips embraced in a kiss.

"I love you, Mike."

We kissed long, hard, and passionately. Afterward, she sensually asked, "How does your head feel?"

"After all that has happened in the past few hours, I don't even remember if I ever had a head."

"We would have gotten a doctor, but my mother was in a rush to get to Panama, so she let my sister care for you since she's a nurse. Hold still and let me take a look at it." She took off the bandage and said, "Ah, it's just a little scar now. I don't think you'll die."

"Well, thanks a lot, Doctor. How much do I owe you?"

"Oh, shut up, stupid, and kiss me."

The gaze of her hazel eyes pierced my soul, while the warmth of her lustful, luscious body set my masculinity ablaze. I behaved as would a schoolboy afflicted with roaming hands disease on his first date. In the midst of the passion, I heard her say, "Porque te quirro tanto no se pero te quierro mucho!"

Curiosity got the better of me and gave me cause to query. "Yeah, that's heavy. Now how about telling me what you said?"

"I said, 'Why do I love you so much? I don't know, but I love you.'"

"Oh, is that right?"

"Yes! Mike, do you know what we are?"

Perplexed and full of thought, I responded, "Huh, no. Tell me!"

"We are lovers, and lovers are loud, crazy people."

"That's nice," I said with a smile on my face.

"Tu eres mi vida," she said.

"I won't even ask you what you said this time. Instead, I'll just kiss you and tell you how much I love you."

And with that, I gently laid her head back onto the white sandy beach where upon we participated in beautiful lovemaking before the gods.

CHAPTER VI

Meet the Aguilars

Upon returning to the yacht, we found that Anita's family had been awaiting our return for some time. Mr. Aguilar was a stern-looking gentleman. His square face and broad shoulders told me that this was a man you did not want to cross. As we stepped onboard, there he stood with disapproval of me written all over his face and with a rather rigid-looking, gun-toting, two-hundred pound, muscle-bound dude standing beside him.

Mr. Aguilar briefly spoke in Spanish to Anita while giving me the look of death. Anita defiantly took hold of my hand as she introduced me to him as Michael Anthony. He let me know with his eyes that he was not pleased to meet me, but he shook my hand any way. After they exchanged a few words of Spanish that didn't sound very endearing, he led us below decks to meet Mrs. Aguilar. His silent, two-hundred pound, muscle-bound friend followed. (To look at this cat, you would swear that he only ate steroids and that he hadn't had any pussy in years.)

We found Mrs. Aguilar enjoying a tall, cool drink and talking with her daughter, Mary, in the saloon. When my eyes met hers, I was taken aback by her very austere but cordial manner. After a few words in Spanish to her husband and Anita, she spoke to me. "Well, it seems as though you and Anita have been getting along just fine. I'm Anita's mother and this is her sister, Mary, and you are?"

"Michael Anthony," I said as I extended my arm to shake her hand. She coldly declined the hand shake but offered me a seat. Anita clung to me as if her life depended on it as she sat in chair beside mine. Mr. Aguilar left to talk with the captain, but his two-hundred pound, muscle-bound friend stayed watching me with a look that said, "Don't move or you are dead".

"Eh, yes, Mr. Anthony. It's strange, but I think I've heard of you before." Her English was without any accent.

"I hardly think so, Mrs. Aguilar. You see, I'm a traveler and the places I've been are quite exotic and out of the way and seldom have I ever stayed in any one place long enough to acquire any notoriety."

"Well, maybe I'm mistaken, but I think Anita has spoken of you often. Won't you have something to drink?"

"No, thank you."

Mrs. Aguilar was truly the family's matriarch. "Annie, we received a call from Frank today, and he had a lot to tell your father and me about Mr. Anthony here. Or should I call you Mr. Cole?" The expression on her face changed from cordial to disparagement. "You are a fraud, sir, and the federal authorities will deal with you tomorrow. I'll have you know that you cannot leave this yacht. If you'll pardon me, I'm tired, so I think I'll go to bed." She left abruptly with Mary tagging along behind her.

Anita looked at me with shock. "Michael, what is this all about?"

"'Nita, there is something I should tell you."

"Yes?" she said with a look of sorrow in her eyes.

"Look, eh, if I'm right, Frank told your parents that I killed Michael Anthony."

She was shocked. After some moments, she said, "I don't understand."

"Look, I can't really explain because I don't understand everything myself, but I'll try. I saw you in the lobby of the Corpus Christi airport on your way out. I was handcuffed at the time to two guys who were taking me to Washington because I was supposed to have killed myself and a few other things that they didn't mention. This cut is from a gunshot. I was the guy on the bike, remember?"

"Oh, Michael, what has happened?" she asked breaking into tears.

"Look, eh, I love you and I'm sorry to have gotten you mixed up in this." I started to embrace her, when she tore away and ran to her room in tears. I sat there for a moment, then followed her. When I reached her, she was sprawled out on the berth crying. I stood there in the doorway for a minute, then retired to my room under guard.

I lay on my back, staring at the ceiling in the dark and feeling sorry for myself most of the night. Then around midnight, after everyone had retired, the door to my room opened and in walked Anita. I was pleasantly surprised to see her. She stood by the door, allowing the light from the corridor to outline the curvature of her shapely body, as it shone through the peach-colored camisole and the high-cut panties she was wearing. Solemnly she asked, "May I come in?"

All I could do was look at her and wonder why my guard didn't object to her presence. She closed the door and after a couple of steps crawled into the berth with me and placed her hand on my bare chest. The warmth of her body excited me. Fondling her breasts and kissing her soft, moist lips made me forget about my gun-toting, muscle-bound guard.

"'Nita, I'll never leave you again. Never!" I whispered in her ear as my fingers explored her pubis.

CHAPTER VII

Rude Awakening

When I awakened, I found myself alone, lying on a round bed covered with white fur. I quickly sat up and looked for Anita, but she was nowhere to be seen. I began to get angry. As I sat up and looked around, I saw that the room was soundproof and that the decor was done in black and white. In front of me was a curious sight—nine television screens (one big screen and four smaller ones on both sides of it) all displaying the same aquatic scene in living color. Coupled with the scenes on the TVs was the sound of the ocean all around me. It was hypnotic and relaxing, but I got to my feet and looked for the door.

Once out of the room, I found a long dim corridor which resembled that of a ship. While I quickly walked through the corridor, I got the sense that I was moving. When I arrived at the end of the corridor, I found a heavy steel door. I hesitated opening it, but once opened, I said, "I can't believe it! It's all a dream."

I realized that I was in a submarine and at the controls were four of the loveliest women I'd ever seen. The women were of four different races. One was black, another Hispanic, another oriental, and the other white. I recognized the white woman as the stewardess onboard the plane.

"Les! Girls, he's awake!" said the oriental as she happily approached me. The others followed, displaying the same glee. I was speechless. They guided me to a comfortable leather seat in the middle of the room and in front of the room was an enormous TV screen displaying a forward view of our surroundings: the ocean. It was akin to sitting in the captain's chair onboard the Nautilus or the Seaview or the starship Enterprise.

I had sat down no more than a couple of minutes when I jumped to my feet, pushing the women back and yelling angrily, "Wait just a goddamn minute! I want to know what the hell is going on. Who are you people and where is Anita? Now start answering and I mean now!"

"Les," the women said together, "what's wrong with—"

"And my name isn't Les!"

The women were quiet for a minute and just looked at me. Then the oriental spoke, "Well, if your name isn't Les, what is it?"

"I'm Michael Anthony, so don't call me Les."

"Girls, they've brainwashed him," the black said as she reached for some kind of gun, which happened to be lying atop the counter near her. "Step aside, he's dangerous."

Bang!

CHAPTER VIII

Your Name Is Les Cole

The following account of what happened to me is somewhat sketchy. You see, when I opened my eyes, I found myself restrained somehow, but I felt like I was floating in a dark room. I strongly suspect that I was in a sensory deprivation chamber or a computer-generated virtual environment. Anyway, as I floated there trying to remember what had happened to me and who I was, a disembodied voice suddenly began to speak, "Your name is Les Cole. You are the originator of Traitors Inc. You formed Traitors Inc. for the purpose of making the governments of the world realize the benefits of working together in peace with one another. You were born in Simi, California." As the voice spoke, pictures of people and places flashed before me.

"You lived there until you moved to Washington, DC, to attend Howard University at the age of nineteen. You graduated at the top of your class from Howard and went into the Marine Corps as a first lieutenant at the age of twenty-one. You were sent to fight in Vietnam, where you met Sueies. Sueies is French-Vietnamese. She was with the Popular Forces, Viet-Cong. Now she is part of Traitors Inc.

"Sueies: born in Quang Tri providence of Vietnam. Height: five feet and five inches. Weight: 110 pounds. Eyes: green. Hair: black. Expertise: explosives and sabotage.

"After you were honorably discharged from the Marine Corps, you were accepted by the Central Intelligence Agency or CIA. You were sent on an assignment to Biafra, Africa, where you met Ikenga. Ikenga is African. She was working for Military Intelligence, Section 5, MI5. Now she is part of Traitors Inc.

"Ikenga: born in Biafra. Height: five feet and eight inches. Weight: 122 pounds. Eyes: brown. Hair: brown. Expertise: electronics and communications.

"You were transferred to the National Security Agency or NSA after you successfully thwarted the assassination of the Soviet president in Kazakhstan, where you met Donzi. Donzi is Russian. She was working for the Narodni Komissarat Vnutrennykh Del—Soviet People's Comissariat of Internal Affairs—or NKVD. Now she is part of Traitors Inc.

"Donzi: born in Moscow. Height: five feet and nine inches. Weight: 127 pounds. Eyes: blue. Hair: platinum blond. Expertise: assassination and nuclear, biological, and chemical, or NBC, warfare.

"Your first assignment with NSA sent you to Mexico City, Mexico, where you met Miranda. Miranda is Cuban. She was working for the Mexican government. Now she is part of Traitors Inc.

"Miranda: born in Havana. Height: five feet and eight inches. Weight: 123 pounds. Eyes: brown. Hair: red. Expertise: counter espionage and transportation.

"Sueies, Ikenga, Donzi, and Miranda are affectionately known as the Vice Squad. Your last assignment with Traitors Inc. sent you to Sidney, Australia, where you killed Michael Anthony, a CIA operative. You stopped Anthony from defecting to the USSR carrying top-level military secrets, but you were captured by NSA operatives during your escape."

I listened to the voice repeat this information over and over for what seemed like years. Then it stopped as abruptly as it began. At the moment the voice stopped talking, I felt something sting me in the arm and I blacked out.

CHAPTER IX

Come to My Senses

At first everything was blurred, but it wasn't long before my eyes could focus on the surroundings. I found myself literally surrounded by beautiful, sleeping female bodies. The enormous bed was round and covered with blue fur. The entire room was blue. I kissed Donzi tenderly and said, "Donzi! Donzi, wake up!"

She reluctantly opened her eyes and said, "Les, how do you feel?"

"How do I feel? I feel fine!"

"Girls, wake up! Wake up!" Donzi said happily while stretching long and cat-like.

After a few yawns and some stretching I said, "Ladies, before you say or ask me anything, I want you to know that I'm fine and I want to know what happened to me after I was captured by the agency."

Miranda spoke first.

"Well, we followed you and the two agents to Corpus Christi, where Ikenga shot one of the agents and you escaped. We tried to get you by the use of a copter, but we lost you when you dropped into the bay. We found you again off the coast of Panama onboard the Aguilar's yacht."

"Who are the Aguilars, and what was I doing there?" I asked.

"We don't know that much about them," Ikenga spoke up, "but they apparently saved you from drowning."

"Well," Sueies took over, "when we located you, we put every-one to sleep onboard the yacht, got you onboard the sub, and pro-ceeded to Alpha II. On our way to the underwater station, we found out that you had been brainwashed. We had to use the Taser gun to subdue you. When we got to Alpha II, we unbrainwashed you and then we brought you here."

"Where are we?" I asked.

"Alpha I in the Alps," Donzi said.

"Yes, yes! I still haven't completely recovered, but I'll be all right. By the way, how did we do in Australia?" I asked.

"It was a big success," Ikenga said with a smile.

"Good!"

I got up from the bed put on my blue robe and walked over to the other side of the room. The women were on their way out when Donzi said, "We're going to the control chamber to monitor the news and find out what's going on around the world. You just rest and be good."

"Yeah, great," I said.

After the ladies left, I turned and faced the bed. I was pleasantly surprised to find Sueies lying there half nude. She looked at me and said, "Ong menh gioi cho?"

"I'm fine and you?"

"Toi manh nhu thuong."

"Now that we know you're fine, how about telling me why you didn't leave with the others and why are you speaking Vietnamese?"

"Well, I just wanted to keep you company and I like to mess up your mind," she said with a smile.

"You want to mess up my mind with the language or by keeping my company?"

"With both, Les, so why don't you come over here and let me finish what I've started."

"Well, if you—"

"Come here!" she interrupted, purring seductively. The next thing I realized was that I was on my back and Sueies was atop me. "Oh, Les, I have missed you so," she purred in my ear.

Swiftly, her lips covered mine and her tongue began to explore the interior of my mouth. Our tongues met and began the dance of sex. Shortly after, her tongue quickly left me longing for more. I put my arms around her and started to roll her onto her back when she stopped me and said, "You just lie there and relax. Let me take care of you this once."

Needless to say, I didn't move. Sueies started kissing my face all over and began to move her lusty lips down my body. She was kissing and licking me all over. "You taste so good!" By now she was suckling my left nipple while fondling my right nipple with the fingers of her left hand. She was creating glorious sensations throughout my body. I just closed my eyes and enjoyed. When she switched sides and repeated what she had done, I was in heaven.

Sueies moved lower and lower on my body, returning to my nipples every few kisses. By now I was fully erect. Eventually, in what seemed an eternity of anticipation, she reached my loins and began to explore with her mouth and one hand while the other titillated my chest. Her mouth and that glorious tongue quickly began to work her magic. As Sueies's mouth closed around me, I was way beyond heaven and going to hell fast in a hand basket. Up and down she went on all sides with her tongue and fingers.

Just as I thought, *I can't take any more of this*, she stopped. I slowly opened my eyes to see what was happening. She began to mount me and purred, "Okay, big boy, let's ride!" My loins were encased inside of her completely, and I had no choice but to move in sync with her and let her have her way. She rode me like I was her stallion. It wasn't long before we both exploded at the same time. As I erupted like a super volcano, she became a violent 10.1 earthquake of love, causing her to finally collapse and melt atop me. All I could do was to hold her tenderly and go to sleep.

CHAPTER X

Living the Life

That evening, we all dined together in a beautiful, ultramodern dining room. The white furniture stood out against the deep red walls. The meal was Bobbie Flay delicious and the company divine.

Toward the end of the meal, I suggested, "Ladies, I feel we have been working too hard, entirely too hard. So I have decided that we just relax for a week or so and enjoy ourselves."

"Hey, I think that's a great idea," said Donzi. "What do the rest of you think?"

"Yeah!" they said in unison.

"Okay, in that, we are in agreement, and I'm finished eating. I'm going to the study to read a good book," I said.

"Les?" Ikenga asked sweetly as I headed for the study.

"Yes?" I stopped just as I was about to walk through the doorway.

"I trust you haven't forgotten."

"Forgotten? Forgotten what?"

"Remember that chess game we started a week ago and never finished."

"Hey, now you know I couldn't forget that, especially when I was winning," I said smiling.

"No, I wouldn't say that."

"Come on, we'll see," I replied smugly.

After playing for an hour and having the game end in a stalemate, I said, "Look, Ikenga, let's call it a night."

"That's fine with me. I'll give you a back rub to help you relax."

The trek to my bedroom was short and uneventful. Once there, she helped me out of my clothes. After she had finished, I did the same for her. I found touching her to be a serious turn on. I took her into my arms. My hands were on the slimness of her waist and slowly they moved down over the curve of smooth, firm hips. Up close, I could smell the faint seductive fragrance of her perfumed hair. It was not long before the tissue paper undies she was wearing came off and her nude body was pressed firmly against mine. She moaned slightly as my lips softly caressed her right nipple. For some reason, I never did get my back rubbed that night, but by morning, I was very relaxed.

Later that afternoon, after a superb lunch of escargot, Donzi told me that she had a surprise for me back in my room. As we entered the room, I looked around seeing nothing different other than the bed having fresh sheets on it. I looked at Donzi puzzled and she replied, "It is in the fridge." She walked to a panel in the wall and touched a button and the panel opened showing a full-size refrigerator-freezer. "Les, I know how much you love sundaes, especially after snails, so I put some things in here for us to share. The other girls don't eat ice cream." She opened the fridge and pulled out chocolate sauce, a jar of strawberry preserves, and some whipped cream. Out of the freezer came two bowls with spoons that each had scoops of chocolate and vanilla ice cream in them.

"Donzi, this is wonderful, thank you."

"My pleasure, Les. This is a little afternoon delight that I love to share with you. Dang, can you help me open these?" She was holding the bottle of chocolate sauce. I took the top off and then the little silver seal, and she squeezed it getting chocolate sauce on my hand. "Oops, I guess I am going to have to lick it off." After she licked it off my hand, I opened the jar of preserves and we made our sundaes.

As I was putting the whipped cream on, I jokingly put a dab on her nose. "That is what you get for the chocolate," I laughed. She looked at me and the next thing I knew there was chocolate sauce, preserves, whipped cream, and ice cream all over us and the table.

"Les, I need a shower now to wash this stuff out of my hair." She stood up, grabbed my hand, and led me into the bathroom. She reached in, turned on the shower, and pulled me into it, clothes and all. We played like a couple of children in the water for a few seconds, and she took off her shirt and helped me with mine. Then came the pants and underwear that somehow had preserves all over them. Donzi grabbed the soap and washcloth and started to wash us both. "Will you do my back?" she asked seductively.

"Sure." As I finished her back, she turned around (her large breasts begging me to caress and fondle them) and put me up against the wall and began to kiss me. I dropped the washcloth, grabbed her, and kissed her back. Somehow we changed positions and her back was now up against the wall, and our hands were all over the place exploring every curve, nook, and cranny. The bathroom was good and steamy. After the water became cold, I slipped out of her and said, "That was some afternoon delight." We both laughed, stepped out of the shower, dried off, and went back in the bedroom to clean up the mess. Halfway through the cleaning, she slipped on some chocolate, bumped into me, and we both landed on the floor. I can tell you that a partly naked woman on top of you giggling is quite a turn on. Our hands started to explore again, and needless to say, we needed another shower after that.

CHAPTER XI

Skiing the Zugspitze

The following two days were spent playing and loving. On the third day, I decided to go skiing and invited Miranda to come along. We had been skiing the Zugspitze for a little more than half an hour when we stopped to take in the scenery. I turned and kissed Miranda's soft, moist lips and thanked her for accompanying me, when she said, "Tu eres mi vida."

Hearing her speak Spanish triggered memories of someone else, someplace else, saying the same thing, but where and who? I asked her to repeat it and she did. I strained to remember. Faces, sounds, fragrances, and more flashed across my mind's eye. It was dizzying, but I began to remember. I began to remember everything and the stress of remembering was so exhausting that I fell to my knees and blacked out.

I slowly opened my eyes to the blue color scheme of the bedroom I first found myself in some days ago. On the periphery of my vision, I could see them—the four beautiful women I had come to know and admire intimately. As I laid there in the blue fur gathering my thoughts, I heard Donzi call my name, "Les?"

"I've got to get back!" I said while quickly sitting up on the bed. It was then that I felt the slitting pain of a headache. It was all I could do to sit up.

"Les, calm down. Now what do you mean you've got to get back? Get back to where?" Donzi asked while Ikenga tried to restrain and comfort me.

"What's wrong, Les?" Miranda asked in a very concerned way.

"Look, I remember everything!" For a moment, Donzi looked at me in a questioning way. "We've got to stop the assassination of our control. Anita Aguilar is a trained assassin. I don't know who she works for, but I do know that we've got to stop her from killing the president of the United States. What is the date?"

"It's the fifteenth of February," Sueies responded.

"We've got to go now before she leaves for Washington. She's supposed to assassinate him on the seventeenth," I said while slowly getting out of bed.

At first they just looked at me in disbelief as I rummaged through a nearby closet for something to wear. "How do you know this?" asked Donzi.

I stopped my rummaging and gave her a stern look and commanded, "Don't ask questions, you're just wasting time. Ikenga, get to the control chamber and get in touch with control and warn him just in case."

"Okay, but—"

I interrupted Ikenga and commanded, "No buts, I've got one already. Now go! Miranda, get the jet ready for takeoff!"

As Ikenga and Miranda were on their way out the door, Sueies asked, "Where are we going?"

"El Campo! I want you and Donzi to get the special parachutes ready for use. I've got a feeling we're going to have trouble. Now hurry, I want to be in the air in fifteen minutes. I'll meet you in the hanger."

After they had all left, I walked over to the chest of drawers, looked into the mirror, and confronted myself, "Well, Mike, now that you are yourself again, what the hell are you going to do when you get to El Campo? Even if you do manage to get to Anita without being captured or killed, what are you going to do afterward? You're the only guy I know that can get yourself into a fix like this."

I slammed my fist onto the chest of drawers and declared, "I love Anita, and if I have to go through hell and high water to be with her again, I will! Goddammit, I will."

CHAPTER XII

Fuck You

It was only a matter of an hour, traveling at a speed greater than Mach four, before we found ourselves passing over the eastern coast of America. The advanced stealth technology of the plane allowed us to enter US air space undetected. Some ten minutes later, we were flying over El Campo, Texas. While circling over El Campo, I ordered the girls to land at a designated spot on the outskirts of El Campo and for Miranda to stay with the plane. On the second pass over the center of town, I jumped from the plane some thirty thousand feet above the ground. It was a high altitude, low open parachute jump (HALO). At ten thousand feet, I deployed my cloud parachute.

As I floated down, I could hear a group of fighter jets zooming overhead in pursuit of the girls. I was sure no one would be able to see me because it was still night. After drifting so far, I detached the chute and activated the Bell Rocket jetpack, which was attached to the parachute's backpack.

After adjusting the rockets and typing in my destination into the onboard computerized navigation control system, which was on the right handle, I headed straight for 111 Alfred Street which is where 'Nita once told me she lived. I landed quietly a block away in an alley. I quietly gained entry into the house via the backdoor. The police arrive moments later. When Anita arrived downstairs in response to the doorbell, she was surprised to see me. "Michael!"

I grabbed her and said, "I want to explain, but I don't have time. We have to get away from here now. Are you alone?"

"Yes, but what's this all about?" she asked when suddenly there came a knock at the door. Anita went to the door and asked, "Who is it?"

"Anita, it's me, Frank. Let me in." She opened it just enough to see who it was as I hid in the shadows.

"Anita, we've been getting reports of a flying man. We also got a call from a lady who says she saw someone trying to break into your place. Are you all right?" Frank asked.

"Yes, Frank, I'm fine and no one has been trying to get in. So please leave so that I can get some sleep."

"Okay, but if—"

"Yes, Frank, now please go," she said and then shut the door.

"Anita, I love you," I said while holding her tenderly in my arms.

"Oh, Michael, I love you. Please don't leave me again."

"I promise, but now we have to go before it's too late."

"I'll go up and change." About halfway up the stairs, she stopped, turned and asked, "Where will we go?"

"I don't know. From the way it looks, we'll be going from place to place. I don't like what has happened, but I don't know what else to do."

"I understand and I'll accept whatever happens just as long as we're together."

She quickly changed out of her sleepwear and into a pair of slacks and a blouse. We left the house and were on our way to her car. We were halfway to the car when a light from the other side of the street came on and shined directly on us and someone shouted, "Halt! We are the police. If you are armed, throw down your weapon!"

We just stood still right where we were and didn't move until a shot was fired, killing one of the policemen.

At the same time a second shot was fired, I grabbed Anita and hit the ground. Anita asked, "Who's shooting?"

It must be the girls, I thought as we crawled over to some bushes and stayed there while the shooting was going on. Then out of nowhere came the deafening roar of thunder. I covered my ears with my hands to try to block out the sound. It felt as though my head was about to split. The thunderous sound was immediately followed by a blinding flash of lightning. When I opened my eyes, I couldn't see a thing. It took a moment before I regained my sight. I looked around and everyone was gone, including Anita. The house, the street, everything was gone. I was in the middle of a grassy meadow all alone. All I could see were green grassy fields for miles in every direction.

As I felt the sorrow and frustration of losing Anita again, I heard *them* speaking to me. "Hey, man, take a look outside yourself and know that you are not alone."

I stood there for the longest moment before yelling, "*Fuck you!*" As the tears rolled down my cheeks, I fell to my knees.

About the Author

Mr. Michael Anthony Tyler was born in Richmond, Virginia, on the twelfth of March in the year 1950 (he was only nine months old). Mr. Tyler was reared in an environment full of racial and geopolitical fear. Black people were afraid of and hated white people, white people feared and hated black people, and everyone was afraid that the USSR was going to blow up the world. Thus, life was tense and everyone was angry and trying to escape via God, the movies, vacationing, or drugs or alcohol or both. The cheapest escape was the church. Mr. Tyler took the cheapest route when he was baptized in the Cedar Street Memorial Baptist Church at the young age of twelve. At the age of eighteen, Mr. Tyler graduated from Armstrong High School in June of 1968 and continued his education at the University of Science, Music, and Culture (USMC, campus of Vietnam). In 1972, Mr. Tyler attended Virginia Commonwealth University and graduated with a baccalaureate in 1975. That same year, Mr. Tyler furthered his post-secondary education by attending the University of Agriculture (USA, campus of Europa). Mr. Tyler acquired his master of art degree in 2003 from the University of the District of Columbia (DC campus). Mr. Tyler, a handsome young, mature, and intelligent man of some years, is presently employed as an academician with the Prince George's County Public School System of Maryland. *Catharsis* is Mr. Tyler's attempt at capturing some of his thoughts and experiences during the early years of his life.

CPSIA information can be obtained
at www.ICGtesting.com
Printed in the USA
FFOW05n0622290117